Christmas Treasures

Lisa J. Ivany

Robert Hunt

Also by
Lisa Ivany and Robert Hunt

At Heart

Christmas Treasures

Newfoundland Stories and Christmas Recipes

Lisa Ivany and Robert Hunt

FLANKER PRESS LTD.
ST. JOHN'S
2008

Library and Archives Canada Cataloguing in Publication

Ivany, Lisa J., 1965-
  Christmas treasures : Newfoundland stories and Christmas
recipes / Lisa Ivany and Robert Hunt.

ISBN 978-1-897317-33-4

  1. Christmas stories, Canadian (English)--Newfoundland and
Labrador. 2. Christmas cookery--Newfoundland and Labrador.
I. Hunt, Robert J., 1949- II. Title.

GT4987.15.I835 2008   C813'.0108334   C2008-906463-1

PRINTED IN CANADA

Cover design: Adam Freake

FLANKER PRESS
PO BOX 2522, STATION C
ST. JOHN'S, NL, CANADA
TOLL FREE: 1-866-739-4420
WWW.FLANKERPRESS.COM

13 12 11 10 09 08   1 2 3 4 5 6 7 8 9

  Canada Council   Conseil des Arts
for the Arts   du Canada

We acknowledge the financial support of the Government of Canada through the Book
Publishing Industry Development Program (BPIDP) for our publishing activities; the Canada
Council for the Arts which last year invested $20.1 million in writing and publishing
throughout Canada; the Government of Newfoundland and Labrador, Department of
Tourism, Culture and Recreation.

Dedication

I'd like to dedicate this book to the memory of my two beloved grandmothers. One of the stories in this book, "Young Samaritan," was written using my maternal grandmother's name, Muriel Collins. I was looking forward to having her read it on publication, but she passed away on February 18, 2007. Although she was ninety-two, her death was quite unexpected and we all miss her very much. She was an ambassador of goodwill, touching the lives of everyone she knew with kindness and love.

My paternal grandmother, Sarah Ivany, inspired another story in this book, called "Forgotten Memories." She was diagnosed with Alzheimer's disease, and for the last seven years of her life, her mind was stolen from us by this dreaded illness. On June 9, 2001, at the age of eighty-eight, her body was taken as well. Even though her memory was never restored, she left her family with precious memories of the wonderful woman she was and the laughter and love she brought to our hearts.

Lisa J. Ivany

I dedicate this book to my children, Stephen and Heather, who have been great supporters of my writing. I hope this collection of stories brings them as much comfort and enjoyment as the first two publications. May they be enlightened, not only by the happy plots, but also by the themes laced with the sadness of growing up in this world, and appreciate their own lives a little more.

Robert J. Hunt

Contents

Section II

Acknowledgements

Lisa sends thanks to Annette and Ira Crummey for their invaluable technical and software expertise. It was instrumental in the printing of this book.

Also, to Dean Pelley, a paramedic at the James Paton Memorial Hospital, for proofreading "A Paramedic's Nightmare." Your comments, demonstrations, and instructions were most helpful.

Robert would like to thank Janice Brien, Steve White, Brian Kennedy, Beulah Parsons-Paddle, Glenys Vivian, and Katie McCormack for their generous feedback on the stories.

Both authors extend their gratitude to all the Flanker Press staff for the preparation and publication of this book.

Finally, but certainly not least, Lisa and Robert send a big thank you to the readers who have enjoyed their previous stories, and they hope you like the newest ones in *Christmas Treasures*.

Noah's Song

by Robert Hunt

Begun in 1855, St. Patrick's Church on Patrick Street in St. John's is a beautiful Gothic church. It took many years and hundreds of men working many hours to bring it to life, and the church stood majestically, especially when compared to other churches built in its day. In 1864, nine years after the cornerstone was laid, work officially began on the structure. The foundation was constructed of stone taken from Cudahy's Quarry in the Southside Hills. Unforeseen problems prevented work on the project from advancing for another decade. Additional stone was donated in 1875, and construction began once more. After more than two and a half decades, St. Patrick's Church was finally dedicated on August 28, 1881. It was the beginning of a new religious era.

The church stood regal and proud, waiting for the first voices of praise to be sung to God by its choirs. Many notable voices sang praises to the heavens, but it was not until the bell tower was installed in 1912, and the voice of one Noah Cordon resonated inside the church's walls, did it officially become a truly memorable place of worship and song. The first time he sang there, Noah was only seventeen years old.

I can remember the story being passed down, from my grandfather to my father, about the remarkable voice of Noah Cordon. It was said that his voice was given to him by the angels, and that no one else could sing the way he could. His voice could make the stained glass in the church tremble. When he sang, it was as if God Himself had thrown a blanket over the whole congregation and silenced the people, awed at this wonderful tenor. Noah and his voice were in demand all over St. John's. His fame progressed, and he was soon considered the voice of heaven itself.

* * *

The story goes that while Sunday church service was in progress at Christmas in 1912, Noah simply walked into the church off the street and started singing along with the choir. His voice was so beautiful and carried so magnificently that complete silence reigned as he sang; people were hypnotized by his voice. No one seemed to know where he had come from or where he lived. He would just show up each week at Sunday service, and his melancholy voice could be heard resonating inside the church as people marvelled at this beautiful apparition sent by God. Then, as quickly as he had come there, he would leave, before anyone could question him. Rumours of Noah and his voice went around town. None of the congregations had ever heard such a beautiful voice as his. People from other parishes started going to St. Patrick's Church just to hear him sing.

For two years people speculated about his origin. Word

spread that he had no home, but was a lost ghost singing to release himself from purgatory. He would appear wearing a cloak that covered his face, his head hung low, and he would sing and then leave the church. The people were left to speculate as to what he looked like and where he was from. No one knew, for they would not dare disturb him while he sang, and they didn't wish to stop him as he left church, for fear of his never returning.

The First World War started in 1914, and Noah disappeared from St. Patrick's Church as quickly as he had walked into it. Rumour had it that he was off to war, fighting for Canada and her freedom, but no one could prove that this was the case, for no one knew of his history or of his origin. The war years were a time of hardship for all people. Many struggled to make ends meet, as sacrifice upon sacrifice was made by everyone to help the war effort.

Some said that Noah had gone to war with the First Five Hundred, others that he was at sea on a warship. Many said that he was only an apparition. So the rumours went, until one day, during Sunday service in December of 1916, a telegram mysteriously appeared for Father Hearn before Sunday Mass. No one knew where this letter had come from. It just seemed to be there when Father was ready to say Mass. He noticed it lying next to the Bible when he walked to the steps leading up to the pulpit.

Father looked at the envelope, which bore the seal of the War Correspondence Office. It was dated November 15, 1916. He felt strange as he took it in his hands and removed the letter within. As he read, his face paled considerably. When he had read a few lines, he stopped and looked out at the crowd that had gathered for the service. There was complete silence as he began reading the letter to the congregation:

November 15, 1916
St. Patrick's Church Congregation
Patrick Street
St. John's, Newfoundland

It is with great sadness that we inform you that Sergeant Noah Cordon was killed in action in the Battle of the Somme on November 15. He was among the first of a thousand courageous men who went over the hill and into battle with the enemy.

He was one of many Newfoundland men who died with bravery and distinction. We discovered his body, several hundred feet from where he charged into battle. He will be forever remembered as one of those who died defending the rights and freedoms of us all. May God have mercy on his soul.

He had asked me that if anything were to happen to him, I would inform you so that you would pray for him on Christmas Day.

Major Paul St. Croix
Royal Newfoundland Regiment
The Somme, Amiens, France

The silence was deafening as parishioners bowed their heads in prayer at the sad news of Noah's passing. Tears ran freely down many cheeks as they remembered the young man with the remarkable golden voice. Many could recall the awe they felt at the beauty of his voice as it vibrated off the walls of the church. Christmas Day would be a sad day indeed as they readied themselves for the departure of the man with the voice of an angel.

Father Hearn spoke to the congregation as he slowly laid the letter on the podium.

"I, like all of you, am devastated by this news and I wish to ask each of you here to pray for Noah, and to please attend the Christmas Day ceremony out of respect for him. We will make it a very special day of celebration just for Noah, and we will sing his favourite hymns, especially his favourite Christmas song, "Little Drummer Boy.""

In the days leading up to Christmas Day, St. Patrick's was a beehive of activity as people prepared for the December 25 Mass to commemorate Noah's passing. Special decorations were put in the church, and all was ready when Christmas Day arrived. The church was crowded with parishioners. The choir had been chosen by Mr. Ennis, the choir director, and he asked Daniel Park, his best singer, to sing "Little Drummer Boy."

Mass started out quietly, but soon grew in volume as everyone sang in unison with the choir. Christmas songs were sung with vigour and feeling as the congregation gave their praise to Noah. As communion was being prepared, Father Hearn turned his head, made the sign of the Cross, and nodded to Daniel Park to sing "Little Drummer Boy" to the crowd, as Noah Cordon would have if he had been there that day. Daniel was about to start, when suddenly all the lights in the church dimmed. The candles that had been lit in memory of Noah flickered and went out. Silence fell in the church as people looked at one another to see what was happening.

Then, an amazing thing happened. Daniel Park left the choir, walked to the centre of the room as if he were hypnotized, and stood in front of the crowd. He made the sign of the Cross as everyone in the crowd stared directly at him. Suddenly, all the candles that had gone out started to light, one by one. Daniel turned to face the altar, and an amazing thing happened. "Little Drummer Boy" came flowing out of him like he had never sung it before. His voice vibrated as he reached notes that he knew, in his own mind, he could not reach. His voice changed into the wonderful tenor that many of the congregation knew so well. They knew it was Daniel Park singing, but the voice was distinctly Noah Cordon's. The song jumped from Daniel's throat as he stood in amazement. The people knew that this was Noah's last gift to them before he said goodbye. Then, an old woman started to sing along, then another person picked up the lyrics, and the entire congregation, one by one, started to sing with Daniel as Noah performed his last song.

Then, as quickly as it had started, it was over. The church was so quiet that you could only hear the breathing of the person next to you. A young boy in the middle of the church felt something or someone touch him on the shoulder. He looked around, saw no one, and then started to clap his hands at the beautiful song he had just heard. Soon, young and old alike started to clap, and Daniel Park turned to face the audience and did the same, for he knew that it was not his voice that had come from him. He bowed his head and prayed that Noah had finally found peace.

* * *

My grandfather remembered that day very well. He had attended many Masses at St. Patrick's Church in his youth. He would go there for the quiet, to sit and meditate about life and its many twists and turns. Sometimes, if he listened close enough, he swore that he could hear Noah Cordon's voice resonating as he sat there in the church. He remembers that night very well, as if it happened only yesterday. He remembers because he was there . . . for he was the young boy that Noah Cordon touched on the shoulder. The memory of that night lived with him until his death exactly fifty years later, on Christmas Day, 1976.

A Paramedic's Nightmare

by Lisa Ivany

"Code 10, Security. Code 10, Security," the switchboard operator announced on the intercom of the James Paton Memorial Hospital. Scott Blackmore and Garry Hillier raced from the medical unit to the emergency room to answer the call. Both paramedics were in their late forties, but that's where the similarity ended. Scott was of average height and build with a full head of coal-black hair; Garry was short and stocky with only a thin patch of blond hair that had receded to the back of his head.

As they donned their winter coats, the ER nurse gave them a quick synopsis of the call they were in the process of responding to.

"We have a fifty-year-old male who fell from the top of a ladder while putting Christmas lights on his roof. He's conscious, but complaining of pain in the pelvic area. His name is Cory Flynn and the address is 54 Morgan Drive."

The two men jumped into the ambulance and turned on the sirens and flashing lights as they left the hospital grounds. The streets of Gander had been plowed earlier and

driving was easy. However, when they arrived at their destination, a light covering of snow camouflaged the icy areas
in the driveway. This was duly noted when both Scott and
Garry slipped on one such icy patch while carrying the
stretcher to the front of the house, where several people had
gathered.

"Hi, Mr. Flynn," Scott said when he reached the injured
man who lay on the cement walkway. "Please don't move,
and keep your head still. Where are you hurt?"

"It's my right hip. The pain is unbearable and I can't
move."

"You don't have to move a muscle. Garry and I are going
to do all the work."

After surveying the height from which their patient had
fallen, they immediately secured a cervical collar around his
neck in case there was a spinal injury. They next log-rolled
him onto the spine board and attached a head immobilizer
before strapping him down for transfer.

"We're going to take you to the hospital now," Scott said.

The woman who had been holding their patient's hand
started to cry.

"You must be his wife," Scott said.

"Yes, I'm Natalie."

"Well, Natalie. Cory is going to be just fine." To emphasize his point, he gave her shoulder a gentle squeeze.

The paramedics started an IV, checked their patient's
vital signs, and performed a complete body assessment
before leaving the scene. Once they had Cory secured in the
back of the ambulance as comfortably as they could manage,
Garry went up front to drive while Scott stayed in the back
to keep an eye on their patient. Natalie and her son followed
in the family car.

After transferring their charge to the care of the emergency room physician, it was past 7:00 p.m. and Scott and Garry's shift had come to an end.

"I'm meeting my brothers at Reflections Pub for a beer and a burger. Would you like to join us?" Garry asked.

"Sounds good, but Carly's making broccoli and chicken casserole, twice-baked potatoes, and chocolate cookie cheesecake, and you know I can't resist that combination."

"Sounds like your daughter is trying to butter you up for something again," Garry laughed.

"You've got that right. I grounded her last week and she's trying to convince me to let her go to the Christmas formal tomorrow night."

"Maybe you should lighten up a little, Scott. She *is* seventeen years old, after all, and this is her senior year."

"I just don't want her going anywhere with that creep, Jarod Connolly. That's the reason she's grounded in the first place. She's been hanging out with him and his punk buddies and coming in past curfew far too often lately."

"It's been my experience that the more you try to put a wedge between two lovesick teenagers, the closer they become. It's called rebellion, my friend. Just remember, she'll be old enough to make her own decisions next year."

"Don't remind me," Scott sighed.

* * *

Large puffy snowflakes descended slowly from the sky and, combined with the coloured lights on most of Gander's homes, gave an appropriately festive picture for the eighteenth of December. Scott enjoyed the display of decorations and felt in good spirits by the time he turned onto Sacchi Avenue. This was short-lived when he saw a familiar black jalopy pulling away from the curb in front of his home. Jarod liked to call his car a vintage Camaro, but Scott saw it as a piece of junk and wondered how the relic continued to run.

He parked in the driveway, noticing that it had been cleared already, along with a path up the candy cane–lined walkway to his split-level home. It was a chore he had been dreading. *Carly must have been really busy today*, he thought. The foyer was decorated with greenery and miniature twinkling white lights. The top of Scott's head brushed underneath a cluster of mistletoe hanging from the ceiling.

"Hi, Dad, you're right on time," Carly called from the kitchen. "I'm just taking dinner from the oven."

"Smells great," he said. "How did you find the time to cook dinner, decorate, and clear the driveway, too?"

"I can only take credit for the cooking. Jarod did all the shovelling and most of the decorating."

"Make sure to thank him for me."

Scott had to admit that at least the boy wasn't lazy, although he hated being indebted to him. Of course, he was quick to realize that Jarod was probably just trying to make a good impression so Scott would relent and let Carly go to the dance with him. Little did they know, his firm decision to ban his daughter from attending the Christmas formal had been weakening in increments all week long.

Scott knew he was being overprotective, but when Diane walked out on him nine years ago, he was left to raise two daughters alone. Unfortunately, a fatal accident caused by a drunk driver had taken the life of Carly's twin sister, Allison, three years before. This had a devastating impact on both Scott and Carly, and since that time he was petrified of losing her as well. She was all he had left in the world and he wanted to keep her safe, but he knew he would have to loosen the reins at some point or risk losing her love.

As he ascended the stairs to change out of his uniform

and wash up before dinner, he paused on the landing, as he often did, to look at the portrait of his daughters. He saw two identical sets of blue eyes, shoulder-length flaxen hair, and heart-shaped faces staring back at him with impish smiles. He thought of Perry Roth, the teenager who had killed half of this precious pair. Anger burned within Scott as he thought how the young man had gotten off so easy. He had already completed his sentence and was now home, in time to spend Christmas with his family, while Allison remained in a cold grave, for eternity. Protected by the Young Offenders Act, the boy spent fewer than two years in the correctional facility in Whitbourne. Scott had hoped he would be tried as an adult and serve hard time in prison for the crime he had committed, but that was not the case.

It was with great effort, but he managed to shrug off these negative thoughts by the time he seated himself in the dining room. Indeed, hearing Jim Reeves sing Christmas carols in the background set a festive tone. Carly was pulling out all the stops.

"This is fabulous!" Scott commented on his first taste of the casserole. "It tastes better every time you make it."

"Thanks, Dad. Can I get you anything else? Maybe some extra bread or more wine?" she asked.

"Honey, quit fussing. I have plenty of everything, so sit and enjoy your dinner."

Scott grinned at his daughter's obvious tactics to put him in a good mood before she broached the subject of the Christmas dance again. He knew how much she wanted to go and be with her friends, so he thought he'd put her out of her misery.

"I've been thinking about letting you go to the dance," he said.

"Really?" Carly squealed.

"Yes, but there are certain conditions."

Before Scott had a chance to specify what those were, he was nearly capsized by his daughter. She raced to his side with such speed and force to hug him that she nearly dislodged him from his chair.

Carly wrapped her arms around him and squeezed excitedly before showering his cheek with kisses. In between each peck, she said, "Thank you, Dad."

"I did say there were conditions," he repeated when she had finished. "I know Jarod is old enough to drink, but if you see him take even one sip of alcohol, promise me you won't get into the car with him."

"Okay, Dad, I promise."

"If he drives recklessly or too fast, then demand he pull over and let you out of the car."

Rolling her eyes, Carly said, "Then how will I get home?"

"I have to work tomorrow night, so I'll give you my cell-phone to call a taxi."

"You've thought of everything," she said, laughing.

The rest of the meal went by too quickly for Scott; he was enjoying spending time with his daughter. It was not often lately that they could do this, between his shifts at the hospital and the numerous school events Carly was involved with, not to mention all the time she spent with Jarod.

"Now, where's that chocolate cookie cheesecake?" Scott asked, pushing his dinner plate aside.

"Coming right up, Dad."

Carly set a large slice in front of her father and placed just a tiny sliver on her own plate.

"Is that all you're having?" he asked.

"I want to make sure I can still fit into my new dress for tomorrow night."

Scott had never seen Carly give up dessert for any

reason, and she never put an extra ounce on her slender figure. He knew that, as content as he was to linger over dinner, she was just as anxious to let her friends know she was going to the dance.

"Why don't you call the girls and finish your dessert later," he suggested.

"Great idea!"

She needed no further coaxing, and flew up the stairs to her bedroom. He was thankful for giving in to her pleas for her own telephone line because it would certainly be tied up for the rest of the evening. He was happy to see Carly's excitement at being allowed to go to the dance, but he still had misgivings about her choice of escort.

* * *

The next evening, Scott's jaw dropped in astonishment when he saw his daughter descend the stairs in her formal attire. She was breathtaking in her black lace shawl and strapless floor-length fuchsia gown. He made the mistake of telling her how lovely her pink dress was, after which she playfully pointed out that it was fuchsia, as if he would know the difference. Her hair had been pinned atop her head and decorated with holly sprigs, and a few loose ten-drils caressed her cheeks. She looked so grown-up, and he marvelled at how his little girl had become a beautiful young woman overnight.

When he hugged her and told her how amazing she looked, tears formed in his eyes for the other daughter he would not be embracing. He desperately wished he could watch both of his daughters go to the party tonight. Discreetly, he brushed the tears from his eyes before releasing his hold.

From the loud rumbling of the motor, Scott knew Jarod had arrived even before the horn sounded.

"What kind of a guy doesn't come to the front door to pick up his date?" he asked.

"The kind of guy who's afraid of his date's father," Carly quipped.

"I'm not that scary, am I?"

"Well, you've certainly made it clear that you don't like him, and he's not stupid," she answered before speeding out the front door.

"There's one more condition," Scott called out to her retreating back.

She turned around at the end of the driveway with a puzzled expression on her face. "What's that?"

"Have a great time."

She smiled back. "I will, Daddy."

Scott waved to his daughter as Jarod opened the car door for her. He wondered if the young man's act of chivalry was genuine or if it was just for show because he knew he was being observed.

* * *

Things had gotten pretty quiet since midnight at the hospital, so Scott and Garry went to the cafeteria for a cup of coffee. Halfway through their break, Scott went to the back of the room and used the telephone.

He returned to the table with a concerned expression on his face which was not lost on his co-worker.

"What's wrong?" Garry asked.

"Carly's not answering her phone."

"That's probably because she's on the dance floor and can't hear it ring over the music."

"I suppose," he agreed.

"What did you call her for this time?"

"I just wanted to make sure she had enough money in case she needed to call a taxi later on."

Garry laughed and shook his head. "You just gave her that cellphone so you could keep track of her all night. I'm surprised she even answered it the last three times you called."

Scott grinned. "I guess I am being a little intrusive."

The intercom broke the early morning quiet. "Code 10, Security. Code 10, Security."

Scott and Garry bolted from the table to answer the urgent call and ran down the main corridor to the emergency department at the front of the hospital. As they grabbed their coats, the nurse at the desk gave them the information she had received.

"Two-vehicle collision at the entrance to Ogilvie Street. Two people unresponsive and the other four are ambulatory although with questionable injuries. Derek and Patsy are already at the scene in the first ambulance, and just called for backup."

Five minutes later, the two paramedics arrived on the scene. Ogilvie Street was just on the town's periphery, very close to the hospital and right off the Trans-Canada Highway.

The area was lit up by flashing lights from the first ambulance, two RCMP cars, and the fire rescue vehicle when they arrived. Several witnesses had parked along the highway and were giving statements to the police about the cause of the accident. An elderly woman and two young girls screamed uncontrollably when a blanket was pulled up over the lifeless body of an old man on the ground.

Scott and Garry concentrated their efforts on the other

victims, starting with the woman. They discovered she was the wife of the man who had just died, and the two young girls with her were their granddaughters. They appeared to be unscathed, but were placed aboard the second ambulance to be taken to the hospital for evaluation.

"Aren't there supposed to be six victims?" Scott asked.

"Yes, that's what I thought," Garry answered.

With three people aboard the ambulance, the deceased man on the ground, and another victim being given CPR by Patsy and Derek, they were still missing one person.

"Well, I've only counted five so far. Where's the other one?"

After a more thorough search of the site, they noticed a young man with blood running down his face leaning over the hood of a damaged car. From his stooped position, and the hand pressing against his lower back, it was obvious he was in a great deal of pain. His concentration was fixed on the paramedics administering CPR. Scott didn't recognize him at first. Then he saw the vehicle he was using for support, the familiar black Camaro he had come to detest.

He ran to the teenager and said, "Jarod, where are you hurt?"

"It's my lower back, but I'll be fine."

"Hey, Garry!" Scott called out. "We need a stretcher over here."

Scott noticed the damage done to the front passenger side of the car and wondered how anyone could have made it out alive. A thought struck him like a bolt of lightning.

"Where's Carly?" he gasped.

Jarod began to cry at the mention of her name and pointed at the action happening just a few feet in front of them. Scott's eyes followed the direction the young man had indicated and, for the first time, looked at the victim his co-workers were trying to save. Her upper body was blocked by the other paramedics, but he had an unobstructed view of her lower torso, covered by a fuchsia-coloured dress. He felt as if he had been punched in the stomach as the air was sucked out of his lungs. The worst possible experience for a paramedic is to arrive at an accident involving a loved one, and now he was feeling the full impact of such a nightmare.

Red-hot fury flashed through Scott. He wanted to choke the life out of this punk, but his main concern now was his daughter.

Carly finally responded to the resuscitative measures and began to breathe on her own. She was quickly lifted onto a stretcher and placed aboard the first ambulance, but she remained unconscious. Scott wanted desperately to hop on board with her, but his co-workers didn't think that was advisable since the victim was a relative. He begrudgingly helped Jarod aboard the second ambulance and sat glaring at him while Garry jumped behind the wheel and chased the others to the hospital.

* * *

Scott sat by Carly's bedside, grateful that she was now breathing on her own but worried that she had not yet regained consciousness. Just three years before, he had been in the same situation with Allison, and he prayed for a much better outcome this time.

"How could this happen to me twice, Garry?" Scott asked. "Perry Roth's drinking killed Allison and now I may lose Carly because of Jarod's drinking."

"Don't think like that. Her vital signs are normal, so I'm sure she's going to be just fine."

"I sure hope so, because I can't go through that again." Tears misted his eyes. "Why are teenage boys so stupid when it comes to drinking and driving?"

"He wasn't drinking, Dad," a weak voice said from the bed.

Scott jumped from his chair, and a beaming smile covered his face when he saw his daughter's eyes flicker open.

"You're awake! How are you feeling?"

"I'm fine, Dad, but I want you to know that the accident wasn't Jarod's fault, and he didn't have anything to drink tonight."

"She's right," Dr. Primmer said, entering the room. "His blood work came back negative. However, the old guy driving the other car was severely intoxicated."

"He certainly should have known better," Scott said. "Do you have any details about what happened?"

"Several witnesses said Jarod had decreased his speed and was turning right onto Ogilvie Street off the highway, when the car behind hit the gas and rammed into the passenger side of his car.

After the physician finished his examination and left the room, Scott questioned his daughter on the events of the night and why she had been on the highway in the first place. She told him a few people had been invited to her friend's house after the dance to hang out. When they arrived, however, there was a large party in progress and it was obvious that a lot of underage drinking was taking place. She was willing to stay, but Jarod was uncomfortable with the situation and insisted they leave right away, which they did.

"You're telling me *Jarod* wanted to leave?" he asked incredulously. "Why?"

"He knew you wouldn't approve of my being there, and, in case you haven't noticed, Dad, he's really intimidated by you."

"I guess I've given him every reason to be."

* * *

Scott was surrounded by relatives and friends for his annual Christmas Eve dinner. It was a tradition that he and Diane had started when they were married, and even after she left, he continued with it each year, up until Allison had died. He felt it was time to bring back this custom, because he knew how much Carly loved spending time with her cousins, whom she rarely saw.

Jarod was seated next to Scott, and the way they were laughing and joking with each other, it would seem they were the best of pals. Certainly, things had changed dramatically between them since the accident. Once Scott realized the level of maturity and responsibility Jarod had shown on the night of the formal, he felt ashamed of the way he had treated the young man.

Jarod had been discharged on the same night as the accident, having suffered only a lower-back muscle spasm. Scott had caught up to him just as he was leaving the hospital and offered a heartfelt apology and a handshake. He admired Jarod's ability to forgive him so quickly.

Scott surveyed the smiling faces around the table. Even though he continued to mourn the loss of Allison, he felt blessed by the family he still had. It could have turned out so differently just a few nights before. Suddenly, he thought, *If the old man in the other car had such a total lack of judgment, how could I expect any better from a teenage boy?*

"Excuse me, everyone, but I have a quick errand to run," Scott said as he rose from the table. "Enjoy your dessert. I'll be back shortly."

He brushed away the light dusting of snow that covered his windshield and drove the short distance to Memorial Drive. He was plagued with indecision as he parked his car in the driveway of the house and walked to the front steps.

He rang the doorbell and waited anxiously, wondering if he should be there at all. Since the recent accident, his emotions had been on a roller coaster ride, from fear to anger to shame, and then joy. He wasn't sure of the exact words he was about to say, but when the door opened and Scott looked into Perry Roth's eyes, he felt only forgiveness.

Bless Me, Father

by Robert Hunt

Fabian Abbott had been deeply devoted to Jesus Christ since he was a young boy growing up in St. John's. His parents had instilled in him a warmth and devotion to Christian life and love. He had always preached and followed the word of God during his schooling years, and his personality and stance in life had endeared him to all he encountered. Now, after years of preaching, he found himself questioning the priesthood that he had been devoted to for the past twenty-five years.

It seemed to him that he could do more with his calling if he was not confined to the St. Thomas Parish and its ministry. Lately, he was thinking of leaving the priesthood, meeting someone, and getting married. These thoughts frightened him, but the loneliness he endured as a priest was starting to take its toll on him. He knew he would have to decide soon what course to take in his life with the church and God. Becoming a priest was a lifetime commitment, but he wondered if he had that commitment in him anymore. Leaving the priesthood behind seemed his only recourse.

Whatever he decided, he knew that the old saying "once a priest, a priest forever" would follow him for the rest of his days.

He had applied to the church more than a month ago to go overseas to help people in poorer countries, but as yet he had not heard from his superiors. Christmas was fast approaching, and it was Fabian's most joyous time of the year. The sounds, the music, and the revelry surrounding the birth of Christ all made his heart come alive. He relished this time of peace and tranquility, and the spirit of Christmas. It was the one thing that made him feel truly blessed to be alive and serving his Saviour.

He was also about to celebrate his twenty-fifth year as a priest. He knew that he should be happy with his life, but something had always seemed to be missing. Throughout his calling he had helped many people, but still he had this emptiness deep within himself. These thoughts and many others were passing through his mind as he sat in his confessional on a quiet Thursday afternoon. He looked through the curtains and noticed that he had one more person to speak with before he could go back to the rectory and relax. Perhaps a nice meal and a Christmas DVD would take him out of his light depression. He snapped out of his thoughts as a soft voice broke through the silence. *One more soul to save,* he thought as he opened the wicket in his confessional. He heard a slight cough before a young voice spoke to him.

"Bless me Father, for I will sin. It has been three months since my last confession," the voice said.

Father Fabian hesitated before he spoke. "Did you just say you *will* sin, my son?"

The young man shifted in the confessional, and in a forceful tone spoke once again to Father Fabian.

"Father, I don't want to confess what I've done, but

rather what I am about to do," he said in a light, barely audible whisper.

"I don't understand, my son. Why would you confess to me something that you haven't yet done?"

"Why, Father? Today something in my mind told me to do just that. So I came here tonight with the sole purpose of telling you something that I'm going to do tomorrow and asking your forgiveness. Please don't ask me why I'm doing this. I don't even know, myself. It just seemed like the right thing to do."

Fabian had heard many things in his confessional over the years, but for someone to confess something that had not yet happened was very strange indeed.

"Please, my son, continue, and tell me what it is you're going to do tomorrow."

The young man took a few moments to collect his thoughts.

"Father, tomorrow night at eight o'clock I'm going to steal fifty thousand dollars from my father's home on Linwood Avenue here in the city. He has been a drug dealer for many years. I know from the word on the street that he has just acquired this money in a drug deal and will pass it over to his drug friends in a few days. I was there before and know where he hides his drug money. I know that no one is going to be home. Maybe he'll even get into trouble with his buddies when they find it missing. I don't care. As far as I'm concerned, if he does, he'll get what he deserves. I know that a confession between you and me is sacred and can't be told to anyone. So that's why I'm speaking to you tonight." The young fellow took a deep breath. The anger within him poured out as he continued.

"My father and I haven't spoken for nearly six years. He abandoned my mother and me and left us with no money and barely anything else, so he owes us both something for the way he treated us. He's never given us anything. We live in poverty while he has everything. New home, car, money. He's always ignored us, and he's hurt my mother many times, both mentally and physically. When I take his money, it'll be my way of making things equal. It's not for me, Father, but for my mother, to give her a good Christmas and a little bit of happiness. I've made up my mind, so don't try to talk me out of it. It won't do any good."

Father Fabian listened in disbelief as the young man spun his tale. He had never heard a confession like this one before. He sat up in his seat and looked through the window at the young man.

"Son, listen to me. As you know, I can't tell anyone what we discuss here in the confessional. It is indeed sacred, but I can give you some advice. So, I will ask you, no, I implore you, not to do what you're telling me here this evening. Hatred is a powerful enemy. It's not only wrong, but this could be very dangerous for you. If what you're telling me is true, and I have no doubt that it is, then you'll be in danger just by going to your father's home. You're only a young man, and your actions may prove costly to you now and in the future. Please consider this advice before you get too deep in trouble and can't undo something that may haunt you for the rest of your life."

"I'm sorry, Father, my mind is made up. Tomorrow night I'll have my revenge on my father for the years of agony that he's put me and my mother through."

With those last words, the young man got up, made the sign of the Cross, and departed the confessional. Father Fabian sat in silence as the young boy walked away. He went over the conversation that had just taken place. At last, he jumped up and ran to the front door of the church to look for him.

"Wait!" he shouted after the departing figure.

The priest saw the boy's shadow disappear around the corner of the church as he ran to catch up. He looked up and down the avenue, but the young man was nowhere to be seen. He was lost in the crowd. Fabian went back into the church, disgusted with himself that he hadn't acted quickly enough.

He went to the rectory with a heavy heart. As a priest and saviour of souls, surely he could not let this happen to the young man. But what could he do? He didn't know where the boy was from and would never be able to track him down in a city this big. Father Fabian walked back to the confessional and, after closing the curtains, sat and tried to recall what the boy had said. Suddenly, the name of the street the boy had mentioned came back to him: Linwood Avenue.

After a few moments of thought, he knew that his only course of action was to go there tomorrow evening and see if he could find the boy and talk him out of doing what he said he would do. He wouldn't phone the police, as that would cause more trouble for the young man and surely for his father. No, he had to do this alone.

The next day went slowly as Fabian tried to attend to his ministry. His mind kept going over what he would do if trouble arose, but all he could do was put his faith in God to help him through this. He only hoped he could find the boy before he did something terrible.

At seven-thirty that evening, Father Fabian was in his car and heading toward Linwood Avenue. He drove up and down the block for a few minutes, then positioned himself at the corner of one end of the avenue and kept a close eye on the passing people. At seven fifty-four he thought that maybe the boy had played a practical joke on him, and was ready to give it up, when he spotted the young man walking down the street. Father Fabian jumped out of his car and started walking in the boy's direction. The young man turned into an alley and disappeared, and the priest walked to it and peered in, hoping that the boy was still there. No luck. He walked down the alley and was soon standing at a side entrance to a house with a door that stood open. Leaning against a wall, he debated what he would do next. Father Fabian shrugged and entered the house, stepping cautiously into a hallway and moving toward the light of a fixture glowing dimly from the ceiling.

As his eyes finally adjusted to the low lighting, he suddenly heard loud, angry voices. The priest followed the voices, fully aware that he was an uninvited guest. Two people were shouting at each other through a doorway. He pressed against the wall and strained to hear their conversation.

"What are you doing here?" a threatening voice bellowed.

"I'm here to see my father," the other voice replied.

Father Fabian hardly breathed as he crept toward the open doorway. He looked in and saw a man wearing a brown hat waving a revolver at another man, who was holding a silver briefcase. He immediately recognized the young man whom he had followed. The face beneath the brown hat looked very angry.

"Take your hand off that briefcase," he said as he raised his weapon.

The young man made a quick movement, as if he too carried a weapon and was about to reach for it. Father Fabian knew he had only one chance to act. He burst into the room.

Two shots rang out, the first hitting Father Fabian in the left shoulder, the other in the chest, just below his heart. He stared wide-eyed at the man with the gun, who was equally dumbfounded.

The priest stood there for what seemed like an eternity, staring down at the red stain on his white shirt. He tried to comprehend what was happening to him as his hands instinctively went to his wounds. He tried to walk, but his legs wouldn't take the command from his brain. Confusion clouded his mind as he gasped for breath. He pivoted and felt his legs give out beneath him. The young man rushed to his side, saying, "Please, Father, no . . ."

The last thing Father Fabian saw was the young man beside him. He mumbled something before the world around him faded away. The last thought that came to him was that he should remain a priest, but he knew that the choice had already been made for him.

* * *

Six years later, Damien Sparks walked up to the altar, turned to his left, and walked the last few steps to Bishop Arthur Powell. He genuflected, blessed himself, and knelt. He bowed his head and then raised it to look directly at the crucifix. Bishop Powell whispered a prayer while placing his hands upon Damien's head.

"Stand, Father Damien. Your rites have now been administered and you are from here forward to be called Father Damien Sparks."

A round of applause exploded from the chorus of family and spectators as Damien stood and blessed himself. He bowed his head and said a small prayer.

"Thank you, Lord, for this moment. I will always serve you, faithfully till my last breath, as did Father Fabian Abbott."

Damien bowed to the crucifix as he stepped away from the altar. He walked a few paces, turned, and blessed his friends and family with the sign of the Cross. His mind drifted back to the night Father Fabian was shot trying to protect him. He relived it frame by frame, as he had done a thousand times before. Because of his own selfishness, the kind priest had made the ultimate sacrifice. Damien would remember that night forever.

He had left the confessional with the sole purpose of going to rob his father of the drug money he so greedily made from the grief of others. If his criminal friends did him harm because of this, so much the better. Then, as he entered the house, he remembered the words that Father Fabian had said to him in the confessional, and guilt overtook him. He realized at that moment that he could not do what he had planned. He only wanted to speak to his father and to reconcile with him.

He noticed the briefcase on the floor and picked it up. But a voice sounded behind him and he dropped it. Then, from out of nowhere, Father Fabian moved into the room and took the two bullets meant for him. The gunman, seeing the white collar, knew that he had shot a priest. He fled through a back door and was later apprehended by the police. Damien never did find his father at the house, and never heard from him again.

Damien had rushed to Father Fabian's side, and tried to comfort him as he lay dying on the floor. The boy tried to speak to him, but a sudden flood of tears choked back his words. All he could say as he knelt next to him on the floor was, "Please, Father, no . . ." Father Fabian looked at Damien and closed his eyes for the last time as he let out one small breath. Damien knew it was his fault that the priest had died. If not for his visit to the confessional the day before, he would still be alive. After the funeral on Boxing Day, Damien knew the only way he could vindicate himself was to become a priest in memory of Father Fabian. Six years later, that dream was a reality.

After the ceremony, Father Damien sat with his mother, Paula, in a church pew. She squeezed his hand and whispered into his ear.

"I know what you've gone through over the past six years and I know you've always blamed yourself for what happened. I also know that if Father Fabian were here today, he would be so proud of you. You showed him and everyone else what kind of man you are today. Just know that he would be very happy for you."

Damien took her hands in his and spoke to her with kindness.

"Mom, I lied to the police when they asked me if Father Fabian said anything to me before he died. He did. I felt so ashamed of what I had done that I never told this to anyone. What he said to me while he was dying in my arms was the main reason I decided to become a priest."

"He spoke to you? What did he say?"

Father Damien hugged his mother as he said, "Once a priest, a priest forever."

CHRISTMAS TRIVIA

Who Is Santa Claus?

The North American version of Santa Claus came from the Dutch legend of Sinter Klaas, brought to New York in the seventeenth century. From as early as 1773 his name appeared in America as St. A. Claus, and author Washington Irving, under the pseudonym Diedrich Knickerbocker, gave the first detailed information about this jolly chap. He told of a saint who arrived on horseback each Eve of Saint Nicholas.

Saint Nick was catapulted to fame in 1823 by Clement Clarke Moore, who wrote *A Visit From Saint Nicholas*, more commonly known as *The Night Before Christmas*. This tale gave Santa Claus his familiar characteristics, such as his laugh, wink, nod, and shaking belly. It was revealed how he used chimneys to carry out his work, and that he travelled by sleigh propelled by eight reindeer who were all called by name. It wasn't until 1939 that Rudolph with his shiny red nose was added to the team. His creator was a writer of advertising for the Montgomery Ward Company.

The North American idea of Santa Claus was further embellished by illustrator Thomas Nast for *Harper's Magazine* from the 1860's to the 1880's. He created a plump Santa who had a workshop at the North Pole and a list that showed the good and bad children of the world.

The roots of the Turkish version of Santa Claus are derived from Bishop Nicholas, who lived in the fourth century. He was a rich and kind-hearted man who loved children and often threw gifts through their open windows.

There are many different theories about Santa Claus from around the world. However, one thing is certain – he brings joy to the hearts of children around the globe every Christmas Eve.

Through the Eyes of Love

by Lisa Ivany

I hate to sign off, Sarah, but I have to go to work. Merry Christmas! said the computer screen.

That's okay, Clark, I have to get back to work as well. I'll chat with you again tomorrow, she replied.

Heather Beaton logged out of the chat room and closed her laptop computer. She had been messaging this guy, who called himself Clark, on the Internet for about six months now. She was skeptical at first of using the chat line, but during a night of total boredom and loneliness, she decided to try it. After all, she didn't have to give out her address or any other identifying information to Internet acquaintances. She didn't use her real name. Sarah was the name of her grandmother, whom she adored.

Clark had been getting more insistent recently about meeting her face to face. However, she kept coming up with excuses. After six months of chatting, she felt he was an honest and decent guy, but Heather feared rejection once he saw her. She had been fairly honest in her chats with him, describing her long, curly brown hair, rounded face, baby blue eyes, and height. However, she had left out the fact that she was a little on the hefty side, thinking this would be a deterrent to their friendship.

Heather resided in Norris Arm, had lived there her whole life of thirty-two years, and had never married. She loved the tiny community and its warm people. However, it was also a very lonely place and there weren't many opportunities to meet eligible young men. She often thought about moving to Grand Falls–Windsor, to which she commuted each day for her work with the Red Cross. However, with her ailing mother in Norris Arm who refused to leave her ancestral home, Heather chose to stay and take care of her.

She had hoped to have some time off over Christmas to spend with her mother and her sisters, who were coming home for two weeks. With the recent flood in Badger, however, the Red Cross workers were pulling double shifts to help out in the crisis. The residents of Badger had to be evacuated from their homes, and temporary shelters had been set up in Grand Falls–Windsor.

As Heather pulled in front of the Red Cross building, she saw Brandon Mouland waving his arms for her attention. She hopped out of the car, asking, "What's up?"

"I need you to help me deliver supplies to the site workers in Badger," Brandon called as he walked toward the truck. "We've just finished loading the van."

"Okay, let's get going," she said as she climbed into the passenger side of the vehicle.

Brandon got behind the wheel and said, "You may get time off during Christmas after all."

"Really?" Heather responded excitedly. "How do you know?"

"Apparently, temporary housing has been approved for

the remaining Badger residents here in town until they are able to move back home. They'll be moving on December 22."

"That soon?" she moaned. "I can't believe they'll all be gone in three days."

"You sound disappointed."

"No, I'm happy for them . . . really. It's just that I've gotten to know them so well that they feel like family and I'm going to miss them."

Brandon laughed. "You always get so emotional at the end of a crisis."

Heather joined in his laughter because she knew it was true. He loved kidding her about it.

Since Brandon had relocated to Grand Falls–Windsor from Musgrave Harbour five years ago, he was often partnered with Heather for field work. She certainly didn't mind being in his company, because of his wonderful sense of humour and caring nature. He was one year her senior and, although he was also single and, in her mind, had the looks of Adonis, she never permitted herself to think of him as anything more than just a friend and co-worker.

"So, have you heard from that Clark fellow lately?" Brandon asked. He was the only person Heather trusted with her online connection.

"Yes, I was chatting with him this morning before coming to work."

"Is he still wanting to meet you in person?"

"Yeah," she replied sadly.

"Heather, why don't you give this guy a chance?" he implored. "Why not go to dinner with him and see what he's like? You'll never know if you don't give it a chance, and you may be letting the man of your dreams slip through your fingers."

"Look at me, Brandon. Even though I work out regularly and watch what I eat, I will never be a size three and that's all guys want. If you're not anorexic, you don't have a chance."

"That's not true, Heather. Guys like a girl with a bit of meat on her bones so there is something to hold on to," he responded. "Besides, you're not nearly as big as you think. So, you have a few extra pounds on . . . big deal. You're still beautiful and you need to stop selling yourself short."

"Thanks, Brandon. I appreciate the pep talk, but let's change the subject." Heather sighed.

After dinner that evening, while her mother lay dozing by the fireplace, Heather set up her laptop at the kitchen table and entered the chat room. She was delighted to see Clark's name already there. Ignoring the other people in the chat room, they proceeded to talk privately to each other.

Hi, Sarah. How was your day?

It was long and I had to work an extra four hours. I'm just getting home now. What did you do today?

I flew to Paris for lunch, went for a stroll in Germany's Black Forest in the afternoon, and had dinner at the Vatican before flying back to Newfoundland tonight. Just another hard day of adventure. Would you like to come with me tomorrow?

Heather chuckled to herself at Clark's comedic writing. She admired his wit and imagination.

I'd love to go with you tomorrow, but I have an appointment with a real estate agent in Scotland. I'm putting a bid in on a castle that's on the market.

Oh, Sarah, please cancel your trip and meet me at the Steakhouse Restaurant in Bishop's Falls for dinner instead. I promise to be on my best behaviour.

But what about the castle? she asked.

If you have dinner with me, I'll buy you the castle, he joked. *Consider it your Christmas gift.*

Sounds too tempting to pass up.

Heather turned her head toward the sound of her mother's voice calling for her and knew she would have to sign off. When she looked back at the screen, she saw Clark's last sentence, which read, *I'm glad you're finally accepting my dinner invitation. I'm so excited and I can't wait to meet you! See you at the Steakhouse 7:00 p.m. tomorrow evening.*

She didn't realize her last response to his line of questioning had put her in a position to finally meet him. She had said it as a joke, but from his response, she knew he was serious. How could she back out now without hurting his feelings? A knot formed in her stomach when she realized she would have to go on this date. Although dreading the ordeal, she knew there was no way out of it.

How will I recognize you?

I'll be wearing my heart on my sleeve, he responded.

You should be easy to spot, then, she quipped. *How will you know me?*

You'll be the most beautiful woman in the room.

Heather shivered at those words, anticipating Clark's disappointment when they met. She signed off quickly and went to her mother's aid.

The following day, Heather was not scheduled to work, and she found herself with too much time on her hands, fretting about the upcoming dinner. After changing outfits six times, she finally decided on a sleeveless black pullover with gold sequins, cranberry blazer, and black corduroys.

She arrived at the Steakhouse a few minutes early and was escorted to a table in a secluded corner of the room. She scanned the restaurant, wondering if perhaps Clark was already there and seated at another table. Seeing that all the other customers were in pairs or groups, she knew she had arrived in advance of her date.

At ten after seven she saw a familiar figure walk through the front door, but there was still no sign of Clark. Brandon saw Heather and strolled to her table.

"Hey, what are you doing here?" he asked.

"Being stood up, I guess," she responded. "I tried to reach you several times today to let you know that I finally agreed to meet Clark. But he was supposed to be here ten minutes ago, so I guess he's not coming."

"I'm sorry, Heather. Maybe he's running late."

"Or maybe he was here, took one look at me and fled," she retorted.

"I don't think that's likely," he said consolingly. "Do you mind if I sit with you until he arrives?"

"Better still, why don't you join me for dinner, because I don't think he's coming anyway," she suggested.

He removed his overcoat and sat across from Heather. When he lifted his water goblet, Heather noticed something glittering on his arm. She leaned in for a closer look and saw a diamond-encrusted pendant in the shape of a heart. Her look of confusion was obvious to Brandon.

He asked, "What's wrong?"

"I'm just wondering why there's a heart-shaped pendant pinned to your arm."

"Oh, I guess you could say I'm wearing my heart on my sleeve."

Startled, she replied, "That's what Clark said in his message to me."

An impish grin crossed his face as he carefully unhooked the pendant from his sleeve and slowly extended it across the table, pressing it into her hands.

He looked into her eyes and said, "Now the most beautiful woman in the room has my heart in her hands."

Realization struck Heather like a bolt of lightning. She held her breath and said, "You're Clark?"

"Yes," he replied. "Are you disappointed?"

"Disappointed! Shocked, certainly, but far from disappointed."

Her heart was somersaulting as Brandon leaned across the table and placed a soft kiss upon her lips. The sparkle in her eyes was not merely the reflection of the candle's flame. Feeling giddy from this pleasant but unexpected turn of events, she started to giggle.

"What's so funny?" he queried.

"I just realized that I met the man of my dreams on the Internet, but he was right under my nose all along."

"And he plans on being under your nose all through the Christmas holidays and many more to come."

In the morning, while sipping tea in her bedroom, Heather sat in front of her laptop and went into the chat room to see if "Clark" was online. Apparently, she had just missed him, but he had left a posted message for her which read, *Sarah, I feel I must break off our online relationship because I have fallen in love with a beautiful woman whom I work with. Do you think she will agree to go to the New Year's Ball at the Mount Peyton Hotel with me?*

Heather smiled at his indirect way of asking her to the ball. She responded, *I'm sorry you feel that way, Clark. I thought we had a real connection. This lady you speak of must be very special to receive your love. I'm sure if you ask her to the ball, she would love to go with you . . . especially if you wear your heart on your sleeve.*

Heather laughed as she logged out of the chat room and sprinted to her closet in search of an outfit for New Year's

Eve. She looked forward to spending time with Brandon during the holidays and especially to having a date for the New Year's Eve Ball. The best part of all was that she would be going with a man who thought she was beautiful.

She glanced at her reflection in the mirror and for the first time didn't despise what she saw. *Is this what love does to you?* she wondered. Instead of quickly turning from the glass as she had always done before, she continued to stare at her image. A smile lifted the corners of her mouth as she saw herself through Brandon's eyes.

A Miracle Before Christmas

by Robert Hunt

Faith can move mountains, if I believe it can, Carter Power said to himself as he dipped his hand into the holy water fountain at St. Luke's Home and walked to the front entrance. He had just come from visiting seventy-four-year-old Henry Blake, a neighbour who had lived down the street from him and who was now a resident in the home. Doctors could not find anything wrong with Mr. Blake other than his loss of will to live since his wife of fifty-two years had passed away a few months ago. He had always been a strong, fit man, but since his wife's passing, he had given up and resigned himself to wasting away. It seemed that now that his wife, Anna, was gone, he no longer cared.

He was a good, proud man, and after Carter visited him, he would go home to his own loving wife feeling sad for Mr. Blake. Carter always remembered him in his prayers at night. The old man's children had all moved away, and he had no relatives living in St. John's to visit him. Carter knew that if not for his visits, Henry would have no one to talk to or care for him.

Carter stopped abruptly while walking toward the foyer; he had to rest on a small bench to catch his breath. The thirty-six-year-old man could only walk short distances; his legs and back put such a strain on him, often he had to sit and compose himself. Even a small thing like walking was remarkable because of what he had gone through over the past year. The doctors were amazed at his ability to walk, as others who had gone through similar ordeals had not been so lucky.

The crutches he used stabilized his body for walking, and he hoped that when the corrective surgery and his convalescence were over he would no longer need them. December 17 was fast approaching and would be one of the biggest days of his life. That was the day he would enter the hospital for the operation to correct his partial paralysis. He had suffered terribly since that unforgettable moment a year ago, when an industrial accident at work nearly took his life. He would never forget the day a machine had fallen on him and pinned him underneath it. Most of the bones in his legs had been broken, and he had three cracked and protruding discs in his back. He had opted for additional surgery now, as the next available time was April of next year.

So now, just weeks before Christmas, Carter was hoping this surgery would be successful and help him walk properly again. He prayed to God every night that it would. Carter raised himself up from the foyer bench and made his way to the car. He stopped outside in the parking lot and looked back at the hospital. With all the recuperation he faced in the next few months, he was still luckier than Mr. Blake, who would probably never recover from the terrible mental strain he had suffered with the passing of his wife. Carter prayed that God would keep him strong and that the same faith would protect Mr. Blake.

He had to make one more business trip to Niagara Falls, Ontario, for a few days. When he came back, he would go in for the operation that would, he hoped, make him whole again. The doctors said there was no guarantee he would walk properly following the operation, but Carter would be satisfied if it alleviated some of the pain he had to live with every day. Maybe, he prayed, God would permit him one more miracle, aside from surviving the accident.

On Wednesday, December 11, Carter boarded a plane for Niagara Falls. He had seen Mr. Blake the day before, and told him that he would be gone for three days, adding that he would speak to him when he returned. Carter's wife, Jill, would be by to visit with Mr. Blake while he was gone.

The flight to Ontario was smooth, and Carter felt an acceleration of peace as the plane prepared to land. This peace was a continuation of the serenity he had felt all his life, from his pride in knowing that he was a good person who had lived his life the way he had always wanted. He had always been there for others, friends and strangers alike. Neither race nor creed changed that. To Carter, all people deserved to be treated well.

The next two days in Ontario consisted of meetings about company changes. Carter's input did what he hoped it would do, and he was glad when the meetings were over earlier than he had anticipated on Friday, his second day, as it gave him time for some sightseeing. He had never been to Niagara Falls before. He left the Sheraton Fallsview Hotel and walked to the falls for a closer look at what he had seen from his hotel window. What a remarkable sight it was! He marvelled at the majesty of the water cascading hundreds of feet into the basin below. He boarded the *Maid of the Mist* to witness it first-hand.

He and the other tourists donned raincoats, and for over

an hour Carter forgot his pain. He looked skyward and thanked God that he was alive despite his injuries, and knew that he was better off than most people. He had a good job, a wonderful family, and, as an executive with his company, earned more money than he needed. Water rained down on all in the boat as it sailed through the mist underneath the falls. Carter reached up and felt the water blowing against his face, and it occurred to him that, in this world, with all the good and bad, the hatred and prejudice, there was also love and kindness. The water beat against the side of the *Maid*, and on over the boat, spraying all the passengers.

Carter had never felt as free in his life. At that moment, he was one with all that was good and kind. He said a prayer for Mr. Blake, and when he did, he felt a touch so gentle and kind that he had to look to both sides of him to see if someone had laid a hand on his shoulder. It was at that moment a peace that he had never experienced before came over him, and he knew that, whatever became of him in the future, he would be able to handle it. When the ride was over, Carter walked onto the platform feeling overjoyed, in the presence of one of the world's great wonders. Something had happened to him under the falls, and he raised his eyes heavenward and said a special thank you for whatever it was.

On December 14, he caught a flight back to St. John's, Newfoundland, and made preparations for his hospital stay. He shared the events of his trip with Jill. Carter made one last visit to St. Luke's to see Mr. Blake, and sat with him for a few hours telling him of his trip to Ontario. He reminded the old man that he would be admitted to the hospital that evening for his operation. Henry wished him good luck and told him that he would pray for a successful surgery.

At two o'clock that afternoon, Carter entered the hospital. He resigned himself to the fact that, whether or not the surgery was successful, he would learn to live with the results. The trip to Niagara Falls had contented him, and he knew that he was making the right decision to have the operation now instead of waiting until next year.

The next few days in hospital were a mental preparation for Carter. He and Jill sat together talking of the day when he would walk without pain, and how he would spend his downtime recuperating from the surgery. His positive outlook surprised Drs. Wyatt and Miller, the surgeons who were to perform the operation, and Carter knew that when he entered the operating room, successful or not, he would face it the same way he had faced all obstacles in his life: with faith. All he asked of God as he was rolled down to the emergency room was that He perform one more miracle.

After eight hours of surgery, they brought him back to his room, where Carter slept for another six hours. Upon waking, he noticed his wife staring down at him, and he spoke the first words that came to him. "I must have died and gone to heaven. I'm sure there's an angel sitting beside me."

As he drifted off to sleep again, all he could recall was his wife's smile as she bent down and kissed him on the forehead.

Off into his dreams he drifted. In them, Carter was walking down a long road by himself, and the more he walked, the stronger he felt. Glancing to one side, he saw a woman he thought was Jill walking toward him, singing a song. He looked down to see that he was walking without the help of any crutches. The strangest feeling came over him, that his legs were no longer a part of him. He tried touching them, but somehow they did not feel real. They felt like plastic. He looked up and saw the road stretch out ahead of him, and he kept walking and singing a song that was not familiar to him. His journey seemed to last forever, and he thought that he was still dreaming when he awakened and opened his eyes to his wife's beautiful smile.

"Hi," Jill said as she brushed his hair back from his eyes. "You seemed to be far away from me by the way you were talking in your sleep. It's so good to have you back. I love you."

It took a few moments for Carter to realize that the white angel speaking to him was his wife, sitting by his bedside. When he regained his senses, he told her about his dream. She revealed that she had been singing that same song just a few minutes ago while he slept. He took it as a good omen for the days ahead. Carter spoke to his wife for another few moments, then drifted off again into his dream world before she could tell him that what Dr. Wyatt had told her.

The second day after the operation, Carter sat up in bed, as well as his sore back would allow, and listened to Dr. Wyatt and Dr. Miller's evaluation of how the surgery went. With a grim look, Dr. Wyatt began.

"Mr. Power, it's good to see you looking so well after the operation. We spent a long time inside your back to determine what we could do to fix the problems that you've had since your accident. It took us six hours to do what had to be done. So, I have good news and bad news. The operation Dr. Miller and I performed was a complete success. We took your L1 and S2 disks away from the trouble areas to relieve pressure on your nerves. After a three- to five-month recuperating period, your back pain will cease to exist. However, there was so much damage done in the accident that there is a ninety percent chance you will never be able to walk without your crutches again. We did what we could, but some things even we can't control. We're sorry."

Carter looked at the doctors and then at his wife. He looked back at Drs. Wyatt and Miller and smiled.

"Please, doctors, don't look so down. I'm sure you both did what you could for me. The news you have is fantastic. It's great to know that in a few months I will be pain-free. To use the crutches for life, hey, it could have been worse. I could have been paralyzed for life. Thanks to you both, I have something to look forward to instead of a life of pain. Thank you for what you've done for me."

When the doctors left, Jill looked at him with admiration.

"Carter, you never cease to amaze me. You've always been a special man. I'm always amazed at how well you deal with adversity."

Carter grinned. "Tell me something. Are you the angel I saw, or was it someone else?"

Jill laughed. She waited until he took his medication before she spoke again.

"Carter, I have someone outside who wants to see you, if you feel up to it. He's been waiting for several days to talk to you, and you might want to have a word or two with him."

Jill stepped aside, and standing behind her was Henry Blake. Carter couldn't believe his eyes.

"Henry, how?" was all he could say.

"That's a good question, Carter. About a week ago I was lying in bed feeling sorry for myself. That's all I did this past year. I started thinking about my wife, Anna, when all of a sudden I felt someone touch my shoulder. I knew it was her. In that moment, all fear and depression left me. I sat up in bed and, I swear, I saw Anna right there in the room smiling at me. She told me not to be such a fool and to get up and go enjoy life for the years that I have left. She said she'll always be there with me and one day I will be with her. It was then that all the grief and anger I've had since her passing left me and I suddenly felt very calm. I rang for the head nurse and asked her when I could leave the hospital. She nearly fainted when I smiled at her!"

Carter looked at him in disbelief. The touch on Henry's shoulder had to be the same one Carter received the day he rode on the *Maid of the Mist* at Niagara Falls. Somehow he knew it. God had worked through him to cure Mr. Blake. The miracle he had asked for himself had been granted to both of them. What a wonderful Christmas this was going to be, he thought as he smiled at his wife and Henry Blake.

CHRISTMAS TRIVIA

Christmas Traditions of the World

Swedish Christmas

The feast of St. Lucia is from December 13 to January 13 in Sweden. It was started by King Canute a thousand years ago in honour of St. Lucia. The story of this Sicilian saint is that she visited the country and was loved by the Swedish people because she brought food to Christians who were hiding in dark tunnels underground. She wore a wreath of candles on her head to light the way, but then she was arrested.

On St. Lucia's feast day, the oldest daughter of each family wears a white dress with a red sash. To complete this ensemble, she wears an evergreen wreath upon her head with seven lighted candles. She serves coffee and buns to family members.

Another belief is that, on Christmas Eve, a Christmas gnome comes out from his home under the floor of houses or barns, carrying a sack with gifts for everyone.

Venezuelan Christmas

Between December 16–24, many Venezuelans attend daily church services in the early morning. In the capital city of Caracas, many roller skate to this service, and many neighbourhood streets are closed to cars before 8:00 a.m.

Before going to bed, children tie a piece of string to their big toe and hang the other end out of a window, and in the morning, if the roller skaters see the string, they will give it a tug.

Greek Christmas

Christmas trees are not a common part of the season in Greece. However, almost every home displays a wooden bowl with a wire laid across the rim, which has a piece of basil hanging from it, wrapped around a wooden Cross. Some water is kept in the bowl to keep the basil fresh, and once a day a family member dips the Cross and basil in holy water. This water is then sprinkled into all rooms of the home, to keep away the goblins who are believed to appear from Christmas Day to January 6.

The St. Nicholas of Greece is considered to be the patron saint of sailors. The Greek legend is that this white-bearded man arrives covered in sea water, because he has been rowing against strong waves to rescue people on sinking ships.

The feast of Christmas is enjoyed after forty days of fasting; pigs are slaughtered and most tables bear sweet loaves of *christopsomo* (Christ bread).

Hiding from Gina

by Lisa Ivany

The piercing clang of the third-period bell made Chantelle Parker cringe nervously as she walked to the gym of Harriot Curtis Collegiate in St. Anthony. This would be her first day back at volleyball practice since she sprained her wrist the previous week. She loved volleyball but feared an encounter with Gina Roberts, who had caused the recent injury. However, she knew she needed to get back to practice, to prepare for this weekend's tournament in Corner Brook. With Christmas vacation just two weeks away, it would be the final game of the year and she didn't want to miss it.

The injury had occurred when Chantelle was hitting the ball over the net and Gina's clenched fist landed a crushing blow on top of Chantelle's hand, spraining her wrist.

"Sorry about that, Carrot Top," Gina had said, laughing.

Although the coach had deemed it an accident, Chantelle felt it was deliberate, having been the victim of Gina's brute force before. She also didn't care too much for the nickname Gina mocked her with.

Since the incident, Chantelle had avoided Gina; now,

returning to practice, she was fearful of another attack. She entered the gymnasium where the girls from her tenth grade team were dressed in their uniforms and running laps. In the locker room, Chantelle pulled her hair into a ponytail and quickly jumped into her green-and-black outfit.

When she emerged from the locker room, the team was getting in formation to play. She saw Gina and steered clear of her throughout the game. Although shorter than Chantelle, Gina had a slightly larger build and her spiked black hair gave her the appearance of a tough character. This was an accurate image, since she played the game aggressively and charged into anyone who got in her way.

After practice, a whistle's shrill sound reverberated throughout the gym and captured the team's attention. Coach Reeves stood at the back of the gym and waited for the girls to assemble around her. When they were gathered, she turned her attention to the clipboard in her hand, which held the tournament's roster for hotel accommodations. She called off the names of each pair of girls who would be sharing a room at the tournament.

Nearing the bottom of the list, Coach Reeves announced, "Chantelle Parker and Gina Roberts." A look of horror contorted Chantelle's face. She would be forced to share a room with Gina for the next two nights! The situation was hopeless, because the coach never changed the roster for anything short of a life-threatening emergency. Chantelle feared her situation could become just that, but how could she explain that to the coach? What was she going to do? It would be impossible to avoid Gina now.

At noon, Chantelle bundled up in her burgundy parka and pulled the hood snugly around her face as she walked to the school parking lot. Although the sun was shining overhead, Jack Frost was definitely coming. She met up with her friend, Stephanie, on the school bus that would transport them to Corner Brook. She surveyed the group anxiously.

"You don't have to worry about Gina showing up," Stephanie observed. "Her mother is one of the chaperones and she'll be riding in the car with her later."

"I wasn't worried," Chantelle murmured unconvincingly.

The trek down the Northern Peninsula displayed nature's panoramic beauty in the form of green-tipped fir trees dressed in garlands of white, sparkling like crystals from the sun's rays. Accenting this was a backdrop of snow-capped mountains reaching to the sky. Chantelle felt her body relax as she stared out the window, and her earlier tension had diminished by the time they reached their destination.

When they entered the hotel parking lot, Stephanie said, "I was wondering if any of the girls told you that Gina was looking for you this morning."

"No. Why was she looking for me?" Chantelle gasped.

"I don't know. That's all I heard."

"And you're just telling me this now?" she asked incredulously.

"I forgot about it until now. It's probably no big deal," Stephanie replied.

Chantelle's fears resurfaced and her stomach felt as if it were twisted in knots. She entered her hotel room and paced the floor, repeatedly twirling her hair around her fingers with one hand and biting the nails of the other – a typical habit when under intense stress.

She unpacked her suitcase and stowed away her clothes as quickly as possible so she could leave the room before Gina arrived. That would buy her more time before the impending confrontation. However, the sound of a key being turned in the door squelched that plan. In sheer panic, she leapt to the bathroom, and ducked inside.

She pushed the door almost closed, but didn't latch it for fear the click would draw unwanted attention. Looking for a place to hide in the close quarters, she quietly stepped into the bathtub and carefully drew the curtain across. With the door ajar, she could clearly hear the voices of Gina and her mother.

"Now, Gina, make sure you do your best in the tournament this weekend and bring home the first-place medal. Your sister did it three times in high school and I don't expect any less from you," Mrs. Roberts remarked.

"Yes, Mom," Gina sighed. "I'll do my best."

"Just make sure you win. You'll have to play harder to make up for the other girls on the team who don't pull their weight. Remember, the Roberts women always win."

"Okay, Mom," Gina responded. "Will you order something to eat while I take a shower?"

"I'm going to dinner with the other chaperones, so you're on your own," Mrs. Roberts said. "Order a salad from room service. No junk food, because winners have to keep their weight down."

A soft thud sounded as the outer door closed, and then there was silence. After hearing this mother-daughter exchange, Chantelle suddenly felt sympathy for Gina. She didn't know if she would be able to play the game if her own mother put that much pressure on her.

The bathroom door slammed open as Gina stormed in. She was mocking her mother, saying, *"Winners have to keep their weight down!"* She reached into the shower and turned the faucets. A loud squeal erupted from behind the curtain as Chantelle was forcefully sprayed, causing Gina to scream in unison with the unexpected occupant.

Gina quickly turned off the taps and asked, "What are you doing in there?"

Chantelle felt like a mouse in a trap and couldn't think of a response. Her fear had reached an all-time high now that the moment of doom had arrived. She tried not to show it, although her hands were trembling and water dripped from her hair and clothing, giving her a look of vulnerability.

As the silence continued, Gina said, "I've been looking for you all week."

"Why?" Chantelle managed to squeak out.

"I have something for you."

Gina left the washroom for a moment and returned with a small box wrapped in red Christmas paper with a shiny silver bow.

"Merry Christmas, Chantelle."

"What's this for?"

"I wanted to apologize for hurting your wrist," Gina stated. "I hope you know it was an accident. Sometimes I don't know my own strength and play a little rough."

With a huge sigh of relief, Chantelle, still dripping, came out of the shower and said, "Your apology is accepted." She saw her drenched reflection in the mirror and chuckled. Within moments both girls were laughing hysterically at her appearance.

While Chantelle donned some dry clothes, Gina headed for the telephone and said, "Winners have to keep their strength up, so let's order a pizza with extra pepperoni."

Chantelle grinned. "As long as there's extra cheese, too."

Easy Money

by Robert Hunt

A multitude of green, orange and brown bills protruded from the open envelope. Gail Parsons scooped it up, flipped through its contents, and put it inside her work tunic. She immediately raced to the ladies' washroom and started counting the rows of currency. The final total in the envelope was an astounding nine thousand, eight hundred dollars. She looked at the envelope and saw that it contained no name. Gail kept staring at the money in her hand. No identification, no name, nothing to identify the rightful owner, just some Scotiabank clips separating the twenties, fifties, and hundreds.

She paced the washroom floor, unable to decide what she should do with this large amount of money she knew had been dropped by someone in the store. Christmas was just around the corner, and with her husband's plant closed and her two children needing so many things, this windfall would come in handy. But would she be able to spend this, knowing that it belonged to someone else? While deep in thought, her cellphone rang and Gail numbly took it out of her pocket and flipped it open.

"Hello, honey," her husband said. "How is your day at work?"

"Just fine, Ron. How did your job interview go?"

"Not too well, I'm afraid. I was told by a friend that they've already hired someone, and I guess they gave me an interview out of courtesy."

"Sorry, sweetie. It seems we have no luck at all lately. I have to get back to work, but I'll see you when I get home at five o'clock."

"Okay, we'll talk about it tonight. Love you."

"Love you, too. Bye."

Gail stared at the money and wondered why she hadn't told Ron about it. *Surely, Gail, you are not going to keep it,* she thought as she counted it again. She had worked at the Quik-Mart Variety Store in Marystown, for over twelve years and had never been dishonest. They were paid and treated very well by the owner of the store. Pete Dobbin had always been good to them, and Gail felt she would have to make the right decision about the money to maintain the trust he had put in all his employees. She knew the right thing to do was to turn it in to the store or the bank, but when she arrived home that evening, she still had it inside her purse.

Ron had lost his job three months ago when the company he worked with had gone bankrupt. He was now going from interview to interview looking for work and becoming, as Gail knew, very depressed with his situation. It was the first time he had been out of work in his thirty-seven years in the workforce. After supper, Gail couldn't keep it in any longer; she told Ron what she had found. She told him she might already be in trouble for taking it home with her. It was a foolish thing she had done, she admitted, and now she wanted to undo it.

Ron sat down and put his arms around her. "Gail, when

I married you thirty-five years ago, I did so for many rea-
sons. One of those was your honesty. I believe you will do
what has to be done. My suggestion to you is to go to work
tomorrow and, if nothing is said about it, then you know
that whoever lost it didn't come back to the store. After
work, you can go to Scotiabank and see if someone drew out
any large amounts of money. Then we'll have an idea who
lost it and go from there. Phone me tomorrow and let me
know how you make out."

"You're right, Ron. I'll try my best to track down the
owner tomorrow."

The next day, Gail went to work and started her day's
activities. Nothing was said about a large amount of money
being lost in the store. During her dinner break, she went to
the Scotiabank in Marystown and spoke to a teller friend of
hers, asking if anyone had withdrawn a large amount of
money within the past few days. Her friend, Bernice, told
her that a Mr. Tobin, who worked at the Marystown
Shipyard, had made a large withdrawal the previous day.
When Gail asked Bernice how much it was for, she replied,
"Gail, I'm not supposed to divulge that kind of information,
but since you're a good friend I'll tell you, if you promise to
keep it between us."

Gail told her that it would remain her secret, but knew
now Bernice was involved in her dishonesty. She realized
that many people can really get hurt when it comes to with-
holding the truth. Gail left the bank knowing who owned
the money. Bernice had revealed that the amount Ken Tobin
had withdrawn was nine thousand, eight hundred dollars.

Gail knew what she had to do. She phoned the Quik-
Mart and asked Pete if she could have an extra hour for
lunch as something had come up. Pete told her that he
would fill in for her and to take her time. She got in her car

and drove directly to the shipyard and asked to see Mr. Tobin. The security guard gave her a temporary pass and directions to the office she sought. It wasn't until she got off the elevator on the second floor that she realized Mr. Tobin was the second-in-charge person at the shipyard. Gail knew that he was probably making about $250,000 a year. But that didn't matter. It was still not her money, and she should return it to the rightful owner. She was deep in thought, sitting outside his office, when a very distinguished gentleman around fifty years of age approached her.

"Mrs. Parsons, my secretary told me that you were here to see me. Do I know you?"

Gail looked at him and smiled, knowing then that she had done the right thing by coming to see him. "We've never met, Mr. Tobin, but I think we do have something to discuss."

"In that case, please come in."

Gail walked behind Mr. Tobin into a beautiful office, and sat in a very comfortable chair next to his desk. She asked him if he had lost anything within the last few days. He said that he had lost nine thousand, eight hundred dollars the day before. He also told her he'd been in Quik-Mart Variety to buy some things for home but had forgotten, because of his busy schedule, that he had been there.

Gail produced the envelope and laid it on his desk. She looked at him and said, "I work at Quik-Mart and I found this on the floor yesterday. Many thoughts entered my mind when I saw the amount of money it contained. I'm an honest person, Mr. Tobin, but when I saw no name or identification, my mind went crazy with ideas of what it could buy. My husband is out of work, and this money could have helped my family considerably. However, that's no excuse, so here's your money back with my sincere apologies."

Ken Tobin looked at Gail and said in a very soft voice, "Mrs. Parsons, the money I lost yesterday was not mine, but rather the employees' money that was raised by the workers to support the Children's Wish Foundation, of which I am the president for the Marystown area. Because of your honesty, some child here in town will be very happy. You have my sincere gratitude."

Gail walked out of his office feeling like a millionaire. She went back to work and then remembered that she had told Ron she would phone him. She flipped open her cellphone and called him at home.

When she finished her account of things, he said, "That's wonderful, Gail. I knew that you would do the right thing. Now, I have some good news for you. About thirty minutes ago, a Mr. Tobin from the shipyard phoned and asked me if I would like to go to work for him, starting tomorrow. He said he needed someone to work in the office, and had contacted Quik-Mart for our phone number. He said that if I'm as honest as my wife, then I'm the kind of person he wants working for him at the shipyard." He paused, then said, "Nice work, honey. Because of your integrity, I now have a job. Thank you, sweetie. It looks as if this Christmas will be one we can enjoy after all."

Gail closed the phone with a satisfied smile on her face. She left work that evening a happy woman.

Snowbound

by Lisa Ivany

Jamie McAllister chewed on her raisin bread and toyed with the last of the fish on her plate. She asked, "Mommy, will Daddy's plane make it through the storm in time for Christmas?"

Before her mother could answer, Ethan spoke up. "You're such a nitwit, Jamie. Deer Lake has an airport, in case you've forgotten, so Dad will get home for sure. Planes take off and land here every day in all kinds of weather." At the age of nine, Ethan tended to speak with an air of superiority to his little sister, who was two years his junior.

Clara interrupted Ethan before he had a chance to belittle his sister any further. "Ethan, don't speak to Jamie in that manner. She happens to have a logical concern. Planes are often delayed due to weather conditions, and we *are* in the middle of a blizzard."

The discussion was interrupted by the ringing of the telephone.

"Hello," Clara said into the receiver.

"Hi honey," John said at the other end. "I hate to tell you

this, but our plane has been grounded here in St. John's due to the storm. Looks like I'm snowbound for the night."

"I was afraid that might happen," Clara replied in a voice tinged with disappointment. "Do you have any idea when the next flight out will be?"

"The airline is telling us that it may be a couple of days, but it could be sooner if the weather co-operates. I'm sorry, sweetheart, but I have to make this call short. There are a lot of other stranded passengers waiting in line to contact their families."

"Okay, dear. At least I know you're safe. That's the most important thing."

John responded, "Kiss Ethan and Jamie good night for me and tell them I'll be home as soon as I can. Goodbye, my love."

Clara hung up the phone, but before she could tell the children the bad news, Jamie came up behind her and said, "Mommy, was that Daddy on the phone?"

"Yes, honey. Daddy's plane can't take off because of the storm in St. John's, but he'll be home in a day or two."

"But Mommy, it's Christmas Eve. We can't have Christmas without Daddy," she said as tears started to form in her big brown eyes.

"Oh, don't be silly," Ethan interjected. "Dad will be home for Christmas. He's not going to let a snowstorm keep him away from us on Christmas morning."

Jamie, relieved by her brother's assurance, left to watch a Christmas program on television. Clara turned to Ethan with a disapproving look and said, "Ethan, you shouldn't have given your sister false hope. Tomorrow morning, when your father isn't here, she will be really disappointed."

Ethan replied, "Mom, I just wanted her to go to bed happy on Christmas Eve. Anyway, I'm sure Dad will find a way to make it home in time."

Not unless he grows a pair of wings, his mother thought to herself.

Later that night, with the children asleep in their beds, Clara made preparations for the next day's breakfast. It was a family tradition to serve brunch cups each Christmas morning. The children always looked forward to the little rice muffins filled with seasonings and cheese. They would stuff themselves on these tasty cups, along with chocolates from their stockings, to the point where they couldn't eat lunch. Later in the evening they would be hungry, just in time to enjoy the turkey dinner.

Before heading to bed, Clara looked through the window once more to see if the storm had abated. It was still blowing furiously, in sweeping curtains of white, so much so, in fact, that she couldn't see her neighbour's house across the street. With a deep sense of disappointment, she retired for the night.

Early the following morning, Jamie and Ethan leapt onto Clara's bed. Jamie squealed, "Mommy, it's Christmas! Can we open our presents now?"

"Okay, kids, go on down and see what's in your stockings, but wait for me before you start on the presents. I'll be down in a few minutes."

They certainly didn't need further encouragement as they bounced off the bed and bolted down the stairs. She heard their loud squeals of delight as they entered the living room below. They were creating such a thunderous commotion that Clara wondered what all the fuss was about. They had never raised this much ruckus on previous Christmas mornings. Without their father present, she thought they would be more subdued.

Clara got out of bed and descended the stairs to the sounds of delighted hoots and hollers. She thought they must be really enjoying the contents of their stockings. She certainly didn't have their exuberant Christmas spirit this morning. Her husband was snowbound on another part of the island.

When she rounded the bend at the bottom of the stairs, she couldn't believe her eyes! There, next to the tree, being hugged by two very happy and boisterous children, was John. Now she understood what all the excitement had been about. When the kids finally settled down and released him, John swiftly walked over to embrace his wife.

She exclaimed, "How in the world did you ever get home in this storm?"

"I hitched a ride with Santa," he said, laughing.

Ethan spoke up at this point, with a smug expression. "I told you Dad would find a way to get home for Christmas."

CHRISTMAS TRIVIA

Legends and Myths

Holly

In ancient times, people believed you would have good dreams if you hung holly over your bed. So how did it become associated with Christmas? Well, it goes way back to the time of the mythical Holly King, patron king of the winter solstice. Holly remained connected with the yearly festival and is still part of traditional Christmas greenery today, along with ivy and mistletoe.

One legend tells of a young orphan boy who heard the angels announce the good news of Christ's birth. He travelled to Bethlehem to see the newborn king and, on his way, wove a crown of holly branches for the baby. However, upon presenting the gift, he felt it was unworthy of the holy baby and started to cry. The Christ Child touched the crown, turning the leaves green, and the orphan's tears became scarlet berries.

Holly leaves have also come to represent the crown of thorns that Jesus wore upon His head during the Crucifixion. One legend states that when the crown was placed on Christ's head, the thorns caused His blood to trickle down, which turned the berries red.

Another story revolves around the holy family's escape to Egypt. They heard soldiers, but there was nowhere to hide so they ducked behind a holly bush. They feared capture because the bush didn't offer much shelter, as it had lost its leaves in the fall. Immediately, the holly leaves grew full and thick, keeping them well hidden. Since then, holly leaves have grown all year long.

Ivy

Many evergreen plants have been associated with Christmas throughout the ages. The ivy's connection has been the most questionable. Like the holly, it is surrounded by legends and myths.

In the Middle Ages, ivy was used to indicate a tavern or wine shop. Not only did it represent wine, but it was thought to cure drunkenness, and drinking from an ivy wood bowl was thought to cancel the effects of alcohol.

In early times, the Church denounced the use of ivy and other greenery for seasonal decorations, claiming it to be a pagan custom. Eventually, however, the church saw the Christian significance of ivy. The plant's clinging characteristic was seen as a testament to the soul's dependence on God.

I Can Almost Touch You

by Robert Hunt

"Let go of her!" thirteen-year-old Mark Lawlor cried as he stood face to face with Darryl Harding, the bully who had pushed Laura to the ground.

"And what if I don't?" Darryl smirked as he towered over him. "What will you do about it?" he asked with a menacing grin as he glared over his shoulder at Mark. Then he laughed at Mark, standing there in his cadet uniform.

"What's with the clown costume? Is the little soldier going to beat me up?"

Mark didn't hesitate. In one swift motion his right knee came up and struck Darryl in his midsection. The bully doubled over in pain as he clutched his stomach, his face registering surprise that Mark had moved so quickly. As Darryl started to drop to the ground, Mark's fist connected with his head, and he toppled over and landed on his back. Immediately, Mark was on top of him, landing a series of blows to his opponent's shoulders and head that left Darryl completely dazed.

"Enough, enough!" Darryl begged as Mark sat on his chest with a tight hold on his shirt. "You win, Lawlor. I won't touch her any more."

From the look in Mark's eyes, Darryl knew he had met his match. Mark sat there for a second, and then slowly released Darryl's shirt from his grip and stood up.

"If you ever touch her again, Harding, I'll make sure the next beating will be the worst one of your life. Do you understand me?"

Darryl nodded as he tried to get up and regain his footing. He was still groggy, and he slipped as he stood up, falling to the street again. Knowing when he was beaten, he kept his mouth shut. Getting to his feet again, he moved away from the crowd that had gathered when the ruckus began.

Mark walked over to Laura and sat down beside her on the edge of the sidewalk. She looked at him and smiled.

"Are you okay?" he asked as he picked up her crutches and passed them to her. "I hope he didn't hurt you."

Laura smiled at him as she stood up and brushed herself off. She felt like a princess who had just been rescued by her knight on his white horse. She had often seen Mark in school and thought he was cute, but now she looked at him in a whole new light. Her hero! He had come to her aid when she needed it most. She looked at him with renewed admiration. She beamed as he gently lifted her to her feet with his strong arms. His look of concern and shy smile melted Laura's heart. Whichever girl caught his eye would be lucky indeed.

"I'm fine. Thanks for your help." Instantly a new friendship was born.

During the next fifteen years, Mark and Laura became

inseparable friends. When you saw one, you usually saw the other. He always walked her home from school to make sure that no trouble would find her. The walk was always slow because of her crutches; she had been born with one foot shorter than the other. He never said anything about how long it took.

In the years that followed, whenever she needed him, he was there for her. They shared a unique bond that they knew would never be broken. Then along came the military, and life as they both knew it suddenly changed.

* * *

Laura stopped her daydreaming as she looked at the picture of Mark on her fireplace mantel, and wondered what he was doing at this moment. This was his third and last tour overseas in Afghanistan, and she had a feeling that something terrible was going to happen to him. He wrote her and emailed her constantly, but to Laura that was not enough. She longed for the day when he would return. She had an ache in her heart that would not go away. And now, because of the distance between them, she realized she was deeply in love with him.

That ache had become even harder to bear as the days grew into weeks, and the weeks into months. She feared for his life and knew that at any moment she could hear that something had happened to him. She had never told him how she felt about him, because she always thought that her disability was the only reason he stuck around. It made him her protector. She knew it was foolish of her to think that way, but she also knew that he could have any girl he wanted, so why should he settle for someone second-best?

All that seemed to change when he went on the peacekeeping mission. When he finished school, he had enrolled in the Armed Forces, following his father's and brother's footsteps.

Before he left, Mark told Laura that she held a special place in his heart, and always had. He said that he was going to miss her very much and would talk about his feelings when he returned. It was a reunion she had longed for every day since he had been gone. Now she was afraid of only one thing, that she would lose him to this war so many thousands of miles away, a war he had believed in and now fought in, a war he told her he had to go to because of his beliefs. He had been one of the first in his company to volunteer again to go to Afghanistan.

Laura couldn't reveal her feelings to him before he left, because it might have influenced his decision. Now she was playing the waiting game until he came home. His return date was sometime around Christmas. She hoped it would be before Christmas Day. His letters said that his tour of duty probably wouldn't take him back home until the end of the year, so all she could do was wait.

Then, on December 18, she received an email from him stating that he would not be back home until January 4. He said that he was sorry he would miss the Christmas celebrations, but his heart would be with her at that special time of year and he would be there in spirit. She was devastated. Not only would he miss the Christmas Eve party that she and the community had planned for him, but he would also miss the New Year's Eve celebrations that they had attended for many years while growing up here in Trepassey, on the Southern

Shore of Newfoundland. With a week left before Christmas, she had everything ready for his homecoming. As the days progressed, she readied herself for the Christmas celebrations with a sad heart. All her friends had husbands and boyfriends to be with during the yuletide season.

The persistent ringing of the phone interrupted her thoughts as she laid Mark's picture back on the mantel. She lifted the receiver.

"Hi, stranger, what have you been doing lately?"

"Oh, hi, Lisa. Not much. I just feel so sad. I received an email from Mark today, and he told me he won't be home for Christmas. The holidays will be a terrible time for me without him here."

"I'm sorry to hear the bad news, Laura. I know how much you were waiting for him to come home. It's not good news, but hey, you can't let that stop you from doing what we've been doing every year since as far back as I can remember. Mark or no Mark, we've always prepared for this time of year together. It's still Christmas, and you know that you have to go to the party at the K of C Hall."

"I really don't think I'm up to going this year without him."

"If Mark knew you wouldn't be attending, it would make him feel bad. So, my friend, you're going to help me get ready for Saturday night, and we're going to go and have a good time, right?"

Laura had to admit that Lisa was right. Mark would be disappointed if she didn't carry on the tradition.

"Of course, you're right, Lisa. I guess it's you and me again this year doing the ceiling decorations. Why don't you pick me up tomorrow and we'll get started at it?"

"I'll swing by around two o'clock. See you then."

The week passed quickly, and Saturday night, Christmas Eve, soon arrived. The town of Trepassey was a barrage of Christmas lights and decorations, and the population was getting ready for the fireworks they had gathered for this evening's event. After the fireworks display, the long-awaited dance was upon them. Laughter filled the K of C hall as friend and foe alike were swept up in the Christmas miracle of friendship and good times. Laura looked stunning, in a long black dress which she had bought during her last visit to Clarenville. With her hair tied back, she was the picture of beauty.

The noise abated as emails and letters from friends and family abroad were read aloud. Bill Pittman, the mayor of Trepassey and master of ceremonies, read many heartwarming stories, and told jokes that had everyone laughing hilariously. He stopped and picked up one more letter. The crowd quieted as he stood at the podium and spoke.

"I have another letter here, for Laura Piercey. I hope that she will allow me to read it out to you folks. It's from Mark Lawlor. We all know that he is serving overseas in Afghanistan, and he asked us to read this letter to Laura on his behalf."

He had read many personal emails, letters, and cards out to all those present, and Laura didn't want to sound selfish, so she nodded to him that it was okay.

He picked up the email and began reading.

Dear Laura,

I've been here in Afghanistan now for six months. I've seen the devastation that war causes and how the innocent suffer so that the dictators of this world may rule. I've seen horrors that the human mind cannot comprehend. I don't want to see any more suffering and death. It takes a terrible toll on one's heart and mind.

For nearly 180 days the only thing that has gotten me through is the thought of seeing you again. Every night I prayed to God that I would live another day, and that I would survive to see my home of Trepassey and you again. I love you so much that I can almost touch you. I breathe it every day I'm away from you, and I promise you I'll never leave again if you tell me that you will be my wife."

Mr. Pittman slowed his words as a calm settled over the crowd in the hall. Laura could not contain herself; tears streamed down her face. God, how she missed him!

The hall was so silent, you could hear a pin drop. Suddenly, a hand touched her shoulder. Laura turned, and was shocked to see Mark down on one knee in the middle of the auditorium.

"I have loved you ever since that day Darryl Harding pushed you down. Will you marry me?"

Laura stood there dumbfounded. "How?" was all she could say as she looked at him.

"I didn't want to tell you, but I arrived home this morning and hid out at a friend's house until tonight's dance. If you tell me the answer is no, then I'll re-enlist and go away again."

Laura jumped into his arms so forcefully that she sent them both to the floor, laughing.

"I think you already know the answer to that question. It is definitely a yes – I will marry you! I never want you to leave me again."

Forgotten Memories

by Lisa Ivany

December 2007

Fletcher Coleman taped the last corner of shiny red paper over the end of the box before attaching the bow. Four festively wrapped packages lined the table next to his miniature Christmas tree, all addressed to his wife, Hannah. He surveyed the gifts and had to admit that he hadn't done too bad a job for a seventy-eight-year-old man with arthritic fingers.

Upon checking his reflection in the mirror, he quickly wet his comb and tamed a few unruly curls of white hair just behind his ears. Fletcher was a proud man and quite meticulous about his appearance. In the eyes of the other residents and the staff of Oram's Birchview Manor in Glovertown, he was always the picture of a distinguished gentleman. The validity of this perception was obvious now, as he donned his overcoat and perched a black fedora atop his head.

With an armload of presents, he left his room and

walked to the main office of the personal care home. Karen Oram was just buttoning up her jacket when Fletcher walked through her doorway.

"You're right on time," Karen said.

He winked. "I never like to keep a lady waiting. Are you ready to go?"

"Yes, just as soon as I help you with these packages."

She retrieved a couple of presents from the top of his pile and they proceeded to the front entrance of the complex. It was just the two of them making the trip to Gander today, which was fine by Fletcher, because he enjoyed spending time with Karen, who was just like a daughter to him. She and her husband owned the manor, but since other employment took Paul out of town during the week, the day-to-day running of the business was left to her. This required her to drive to Gander frequently for business purposes. Since she didn't like driving on the highway alone and Fletcher needed transportation to visit his wife, Karen would drop him off to visit Hannah and pick him up before she returned to Glovertown.

They boarded the SUV, and Karen said, "How about some Christmas music?"

Fletcher smiled. "Sounds good to me."

"I was hoping you'd say that, because I just happen to have your favourite Christmas CD with me."

Fletcher's eyes sparkled as Karen inserted the disc, and they were soon singing along to the festive lyrics with Charley Pride.

With the sun shining overhead and the Trans-Canada Highway bordered on both sides with snow-capped trees, the journey was pleasant and time seemed to fly by. Before they knew it, they were pulling into the parking lot of Lakeside Homes. Fletcher refused Karen's offer to help carry the packages inside, knowing she had several shops to visit for supplies and that, it being Christmas Eve, most places would be closing early.

Sadness plagued him every time he walked the familiar corridors of the nursing home, all the way to the Special Care Unit. It had hurt him terribly when he finally had to agree with his and Hannah's relatives, and their physician that he could no longer take care of Hannah. She had become a permanent resident of Lakeside Homes five years before, and he still bore a burden of guilt. Afflicted by arthritis, he had found it increasingly difficult to look after himself, which prompted his own move to the home in Glovertown two years later.

"Merry Christmas, Mr. Coleman," a voice called from behind the nursing station. "Looks like somebody's been busy shopping."

He shifted the packages in his arms for a better view. "Merry Christmas to you too, Shawna, but remember what I told you. Please call me Fletcher. I'm too young to be called Mister," he said, laughing.

"Okay, Fletcher. You're just in time to have lunch with your wife."

He had brought along a sandwich for himself and would spoon-feed Hannah the minced food of her special diet. It certainly didn't appear very appealing to him, but she had a hearty appetite and always ate every bite. He wondered if she could even taste it.

When he walked into her room, she was sitting in her rocker, staring out the window.

"Merry Christmas, darling," he said, but she didn't acknowledge the greeting. Instead, she remained staring vacantly through the glass as though completely unaware of his presence. She didn't even react when he placed a kiss upon her cheek before feeding her. He unwrapped her presents and held each one in front of her, hoping for some reaction, but she remained as still and silent as stone. Some days she was quite a chatterbox and other days she was like this. He preferred the days when she was talkative because at least she was showing some sign of life, even though she hadn't called him by name in nearly a year now. Most of the time her words were unintelligible, but every now and then she would speak of something from their past and call him by someone else's name, such as Victor, the name of their son.

Hannah's Alzheimer's had advanced alarmingly quickly and it broke his heart to see her this way. He knew he would rather lose his life than lose his mind, and he was tortured by the thought that she surely felt the same way. The only positive aspect of this terrible illness was the fact that she was spared the grieving process of losing Victor to cancer a year before – a heartache that Fletcher was still trying to come to terms with.

Suddenly, Hannah broke her silence with a few mumbled words.

"What's that?" Fletcher asked.

She repeated what seemed to be the same sounds over and over until finally Fletcher heard *read memories*. Her hand pointed toward her nightstand, and that's when he knew he had heard her correctly. She was indicating the blue, hard-covered book inlaid with letters in gold script, *House of Coleman*. It was a lined journal given to them as a wedding gift in which they had recorded the happy memories of their life together. Hannah had the better penmanship, so she had been delegated the task of writing the entries at the beginning of each month, although on occasion, Fletcher would add one of his own, especially if it was to praise something his wife had done. Every New Year's Day, they would open their book of memories and read the entries they had written the previous year.

He opened the book at random and selected an entry from December of 1974.

> Fletcher searched the house, looking for his pipe. He was sure he had left it on the end table next to his recliner in the den, but it was nowhere to be found. It wasn't until he called Victor in for dinner that he discovered the location of the missing item. Smiling at him from the front yard was a snowman, with the pipe in one side of its mouth. When asked why he took the pipe, Victor said it was bad for his father's health. "What about Frosty's health?" Fletcher asked, to which Victor replied, "He'll be okay, Dad. Snowmen don't have lungs."

Fletcher laughed at the memory of that day, and he recalled how he never smoked again, wanting to set a good example for his son. He looked at his wife to see if there was any response to the excerpt he had just read. Her vacuous stare remained unchanged, and he wondered if there was any comprehension at all. *Does she even know it's Christmas?* he wondered.

He read a few more entries before placing the book back in its place. Hannah had dozed off by this time and her glasses had slipped to the end of her nose, which they often did these days. Her body had become so emaciated since the start of her illness that items such as her glasses, wedding ring, and dentures no longer fit properly. It saddened him to see her mind and body waste away before his eyes, and he was totally incapable of stopping.

* * *

After Fletcher returned home, he retrieved one last gift-wrapped package and left his room. At the end of the hallway, he tapped on the door that bore the name MARINA GRAY painted in white letters on a pink wooden plaque. The door was opened by a petite woman with a charming smile and sparkling eyes. Although in her late sixties, there was a youthfulness about her, not only because she still dyed her hair ash blonde, but because her skin still had a healthy glow and barely the trace of a wrinkle.

"You're back," she said. "How is my sister?"

"Today was one of her quiet days, but she was basically the same," he replied as he entered Marina's room.

"It will probably be another week or so before I can visit her. The doctor was in today and said there is still some congestion on my chest, even though I feel fine."

"Does that mean you're up to opening your Christmas presents?" he asked as he handed her the package in his hand.

"Perhaps I'll open one tonight, but let's have dinner first."

Fletcher's stomach was rumbling, and he needed no further persuasion; he escorted his sister-in-law to the dining room. The area was only half full this evening, as many of the residents were staying in the homes of family members during the holiday season. That was a privilege Fletcher no longer enjoyed since Victor passed away. He missed all the outings he had had with his son since Hannah's illness and, even more, he missed the Christmases the three of them had spent together before that.

Marina was his closest relative, and he was grateful to have her living down the hall. She had never married or had children, and since Hannah was her only living relative, there was no place for her to visit during Christmas either. However, the close friendships that both she and Fletcher had made with other residents of the home made life bearable.

They joined three of these friends now as they sat down to dinner in the manor's dining room. Fletcher couldn't help but feel a little guilty about the company of his friends and the hearty meal in front of him while his wife was alone in her room being spoon-fed a monotonous diet of minced food.

* * *

On Christmas Day, Karen had to make an unexpected trip to Gander and Fletcher took the opportunity to visit his wife. When he reached the nursing station, Shawna called him to one side with a strange expression on her face.

"I've been trying to reach you for the last hour," she said.

"What's up? Is something wrong with Hannah?"

"Not really. It's just that she's lucid."

"Is that normal?"

"It happens sometimes, although we don't know why or how long it will last. It varies from one person to another."

Fletcher's feelings were conflicted as he walked to his wife's room, hoping she would recognize him and at the same time worrying she might have relapsed. It was hard enough losing her to Alzheimer's the first time, but to have her back temporarily and then lose her again would be devastating. On the other hand, he realized he should be grateful for any time he could spend with her while she was cognizant. Most people afflicted with this horrible illness didn't get a second chance.

Fletcher stood in her doorway, unnoticed, and watched her as she stood in front of the mirror, brushing her hair. From her reflection, he could see that she had applied rouge, eye makeup, and lipstick, which gave her the appearance of the woman she once was. He was amazed at the transformation.

His earlier trepidation gave way to relief when she spied him in the mirror, and a broad smile brightened her face. She turned and scooted into his outstretched arms.

"Fletcher, I'm so glad you're here!" she exclaimed.

"Not as glad as I am to hear you say my name."

"I was so frightened to wake up in this strange place today," she sighed. "Is it true, Fletcher? Do I really have Alzheimer's?"

He released his hold on her and led her to the bed, and they sat down side by side.

"I'm afraid so, my darling."

"But I remember everything of our lives together. From our wedding day, to Victor's birth, watching him grow up and join the police force. Why, just yesterday, Victor gave me a lovely gold watch for Mother's Day."

"Honey, today is December 25 in the year 2007. You've been living here for the past five years."

Panic was evident in her eyes. "You mean I've lost five years of my life? I've lost five years with you and Victor?"

"Stay calm, my love. You're okay now and that's all that matters."

"I guess so," she said with little enthusiasm. She was reeling from the disturbing information she was receiving.

Fletcher had had five years to adjust to her illness, but it was all new to her and it was making her head spin.

"Where's Victor?" she asked.

"He's on an undercover assignment and I can't reach him at the moment."

Fletcher hoped his lie was convincing and that she didn't notice the sorrow in his eyes at the mention of their son's name. He couldn't tell her the truth yet, not when she was dealing with so much emotional turmoil already. He knew first-hand the deep grief a parent feels on losing a child, regardless of their age, and he wanted to spare Hannah that unbearable pain.

* * *

Fletcher spent the next two days glued to his wife's side, having been given permission to stay round the clock in her room, under the circumstances. He had rewrapped her presents and watched as she excitedly opened each one. She smiled and thanked him with genuine gratitude, and he cherished her animation – so different from when he originally opened them in front of her emotionless stare.

They had so much to talk about, and she wanted to catch up on anything important she had missed while her mind was missing in action. It was the happiest Fletcher had been in a long time, and he didn't want their time together to end. He hadn't realized how much he missed the sound of his wife's voice until now.

On the morning of December 27, Fletcher awoke and quietly got out of bed, trying not to wake his sleeping wife. After he washed and shaved, he dressed in the same shirt and trousers he had been wearing since he came to visit on

Christmas Day. By the time he slipped into his shoes, his wife had sleepily opened her eyes.

"Hannah, as much as I hate to leave you, I really need to get a change of clothing," he said. "Karen will be here shortly to pick me up and she said she can bring me back tomorrow morning. Is that okay with you, dear?"

"Yes, as long as you pack a large suitcase so you can stay longer next time."

He smiled. "I'll do that. And I'll bring Marina with me. She's really anxious to see you."

"I can't wait to see her, too. I just wish I could see Victor."

"So, what will you do while I'm gone?" he asked in an effort to change the subject.

She pulled the familiar blue book, *House of Coleman*, from the nightstand and said, "I thought I'd catch up on some memories."

* * *

Fletcher had just finished packing his suitcase when he heard a light tap on his door. *That must be Marina*, he thought.

"Come on in," he called. "I'm just putting on my coat and then we're off to see your sister."

The door opened, but instead of Marina, it was Karen who entered. Fletcher could tell from the look on her face that she had bad news.

"I'm sorry, Fletcher, but I just had a call from Shawna at Lakeside Homes. She said Hannah had a massive heart attack last night and died in her sleep."

"But she was getting better," he said as he sank into a chair. Even though he had been told that her recent clarity was likely temporary, he had been in denial. He had wanted her to be well so much that he actually fooled his heart into believing it.

His eyes misted with tears and he cried, "I've lost her for good this time."

"I'm afraid so, Fletcher." She knelt down in front of him and held his hands in hers. "Is there anything I can do?"

"Actually, would you mind asking Marina to come by so I can break the news to her?"

"I'll do that right away, and remember, I'm here anytime you need me." She kissed his tear-stained cheek and brushed away her own tears as she left the room.

* * *

Hannah Coleman was buried on New Year's Eve at the Glovertown cemetery, a short distance from her son. Although a large crowd had attended the funeral and then gathered at the cemetery, Fletcher could barely recall a face. The last few days had been somewhat of a blur for him as he tried to grapple with the reality that his beloved wife was gone forever. However, he was grateful that for the last two days of her life she had been happy.

It was close to midnight by the time Fletcher returned to his room. The recreation room at the manor had been set up with refreshments for the mourners and a steady stream of friends and residents had come by to see him. Although he had just been through a very long and difficult day, he was in no mood to sleep. Instead, he pulled out the blue journal from the box containing Hannah's personal effects, which had been sent from Lakeside Homes.

He read several entries, and even though they were happy memories captured on the pages, it hurt that he could not share them with his wife and son. He turned to the last page to take a look at his final entry, which he had written just before Victor died, and was shocked to see Hannah's handwriting. The entry was dated December 27, 2007!

> Fletcher said I have Alzheimer's disease, and for some reason, after five years, I'm better. I don't recall those missing years, but I can only imagine how hard it must have been for him, especially all those long-distance drives to see me every week. I don't know what I ever did to deserve such a wonderful husband.
>
> I've been reading through this journal and laughing at all the wonderful memories. There certainly was an abundance of laughter and love in our home and I pray that I will remember those moments for the rest of my life.
>
> In keeping with our annual tradition, I look forward to reading through some of these entries on New Year's Day with my husband. The only thing that could top that is for my son to come home, but I'm sure I'll see him soon.

Fletcher's tears fell like rain as he read the last words his wife ever wrote, and as the time was now well past midnight, he knew she was there, reading with him, on New Year's Day.

CHRISTMAS TRIVIA

Quiz: Test Your Holiday Knowledge

1. What food is traditionally served in Newfoundland homes on Christmas Eve?

a) Beef stew
b) Fish
c) Jiggs' dinner
d) Goulash

2. Good King Wenceslas was the king of which country?

a) Spain
b) Turkey
c) India
d) Bohemia

3. In Dutch tradition, instead of stockings, children put out:

a) Shoes
b) Hats
c) Soup bowls
d) Mittens

4. The line "'Fear not then,' said the angel, 'let nothing you affright'" is from what Christmas carol?

a) We Three Kings of Orient Are
b) What Child Is This?
c) God Rest Ye Merry Gentlemen
d) Do You Hear What I Hear?

5. Which of the following is not a name for Santa Claus?

a) Sinter Klaas
b) Kris Kringle
c) St. Nicholas
d) St. Clauser

6. Who wrote *A Christmas Carol*?

a) Samuel Clemens
b) Charles Dickens
c) Ernest Hemingway
d) William Shakespeare

7. In a popular Christmas cartoon, who was the green villain of the town of Whoville?

a) The Grinch
b) The Abominable Snowman
c) Ebenezer Scrooge
d) Jack Frost

8. Which of the following is not one of Santa's reindeer?

a) Vixen

b) Rudolph

c) Comet

d) Dander

9. What was the first instrument *Silent Night* was played on?

a) Piano

b) Flute

c) Guitar

d) Harp

10. The tale entitled *A Visit From St. Nicholas* was later called:

a) Here Comes Santa Claus

b) The Night Before Christmas

c) Christmas Wonderland

d) Around the World in One Night

Answers: 1-b; 2-d; 3-a; 4-c; 5-d; 6-b; 7-a; 8-d; 9-c; 10-b

Teddy Bear Lady

by Robert Hunt

Four hundred eyes stared at Sheila Knight as she silently packed the boxes that held twenty of each item. She carefully taped up the boxes and loaded them aboard her truck and closed the doors. When she was satisfied that her cargo was secure, she sat behind the wheel and started the engine. Today was to be a special day in the lives of nearly two hundred children. Today, a few days before Christmas Day, was Teddy Bear Day for them. She had hand-picked each bear and tied a beautiful Christmas bow around its neck for each child at the hospital.

She drove the five miles from her home to the Janeway Children's Hospital, parked in the spot that the hospital had reserved especially for her, and backed her truck up to the door to unload her cargo. Within minutes, orderlies and nurses were helping her bring the precious boxes into the building. Once inside, the wrapped teddy bears were placed in rows on metal trolleys that would transport them to the children on the wards. Care was taken to ensure none were torn or broken on their short journey to each special guardian. Sheila was always the first person to walk the path she had walked many times in her years as a caregiver at the Janeway. Hers was the first face that the children saw as they reached out and put their hands on the precious packages.

The atmosphere of Christmas was apparent. Decorations adorned the halls where she had spent so many of her working years. She went from room to room, and her smiles were reciprocated as the workers walked with her about the wards and offered the gifts to the sick children.

These little packages were special in their own way. They did not cry nor complain, they had no hatred or animosity toward anyone, and they always made the recipient feel very special. The children smiled at her through their pain. None refused her companionship, and none were too sick to turn away a teddy bear as Sheila passed by their beds.

She was once an RN, and now she had found the perfect way to enjoy her retirement. She remembered the first day she had gone to work at the old Janeway Children's Hospital, then located in Pleasantville. She learned the suffering of terminally ill children and had seen many pass away from their illness, but she also had seen many recover. When a child was in pain, so was she. Each loss took a part of her with it, because she felt that each child was *her* child, and she hurt inside when one suddenly left this earth.

With the passing of the years, Sheila became more and more attached to the children she helped through their illnesses. Whenever one was sick, she made special trips, even after her day was done, to ensure that the child was comfortable or had taken their medication, or she read them a bedtime story when others were too busy to do so. She had a love inside her that made her unique among the staff who worked there. She never seemed to tire when it came to the children, and many times her friends had seen her sitting with a lonely child when her shift was long over. She was loved by everyone, and she enjoyed her job so much that she had found it hard to leave when it came time for retirement.

It was at the Janeway, in 1998, that she met little Jeanie Abbott. The girl had been born with a curvature of the spine that most times left her in pain as her little body developed from a baby to a young girl. She was only eight years old, but Sheila saw in her a child who was much more mature than her young years would indicate. Jeanie fought the pain she endured, and hardly ever cried. When she did, she always looked to Sheila as her comfort zone. Sheila became very close to her, and spent many nights talking and reading stories to her. Children like Jeanie were the reason that Sheila became a nurse in the first place, to comfort the sick and dying while they shared this earth with her.

For four years, young Jeanie was in and out of hospital to correct her curvature, and she became very attached to Sheila, who was like her second mother. Her parents were from Botwood, in Central Newfoundland, and they found it very hard to come to St. John's to see their daughter. Her mother took much comfort in knowing that Sheila was there with her at the hospital, and that she was well taken care of. After five years, when it came time for Jeanie to leave the Janeway, Sheila felt that she was losing her own daughter. In the years that followed, they never lost contact with each other, and letters and phone calls were frequent. As Jeanie grew into a young woman, she often visited Sheila at the Janeway and at home.

When the new hospital became an annex of the Health Sciences Complex, Sheila became an integral part of the running of the new hospital. She was the head nurse, but soon her duties and responsibilities included a heavier work-load than ever before. This didn't stop her from putting *her* children first, and she always took on the responsibility of ensuring that the children came first and all else second.

Although she was now retired, she still devoted her life to the care of the children. Her desire to do more and more for these small wonders, whom she always called her "special little ones," never ceased. In retirement, she spent just as much time at the hospital as she did before; she did it without any timetable, and she did it all for the children, always for the children. At sixty-six, still giving her all for the children as she had since she was twenty-one, she felt the sense of peace and contentment that one feels when he or she has contributed to something wonderful all their lives. She was very proud of her achievements.

Then, in Christmas of 2006, the Teddy Bear Lady, as she was dubbed by her friends and peers alike, was asked to present that year's awards to the nurses at their annual Christmas party. She and her husband, Don, had been invited every year since she retired, but this was the first year they had asked her to be the master of ceremonies. She had always attended the parties, as they gave her another excuse to visit the children before the festivities began. She looked forward to this year's event in particular, as some of the children who had finally beaten their diseases were also coming back to present awards and gifts to some of the nurses and volunteer staff.

Presentation night came, and Sheila and Don were given a special seat at the head table. For nearly an hour she presented awards to many of the nurses, staff members, and doctors with whom she had worked for years. She presented new nurses with their inaugural beginner's pins and welcomed them into nursing. She gave out numerous awards to senior nurses and laughed and joked her way through a variety of presentations. It was beginning to look like a night she would remember for many years, and something she would hold dear to her heart.

About two hours into the ceremony, when all the awards were presented and the honours bestowed, Dr. Craig Parsons, the chief of medical staff, came to the podium and cleared his throat. He waited until all the noise had quieted down before speaking to the audience in his soft voice.

"Ladies and gentlemen, this evening has been very special to me indeed. All of us here tonight have seen what unique people we have working here at the Janeway. I am proud to be here tonight and to be able to present these awards to all of you. Each and every one of you deserves the acclamation that you have received this evening.

"Tonight we have a very special guest who asked me if he could be part of this awards ceremony. When I heard the reason he wished to come here tonight, I consented without hesitation. So, without out further ado, I would like this person to come forward and speak to us."

With his speech completed, Dr. Parsons left the podium, and a young man of about twenty stood up from his chair and walked to the podium. He stood for a few moments and scanned the crowd. He then turned his gaze on Sheila and spoke directly to her.

"Hello, Mrs. Knight, my name is Randy Sorenson." He looked at her and then turned to the audience.

"Many of you do not know me, but I am here today because a very special nurse took me into her heart about six years ago, when I was a very sick young man. She showed me love, caring, and the biggest heart I have ever known. I had a severe heart defect that nearly took my life, but thanks to two special doctors and one nurse, who did not know the meaning of the word 'quit,' I am here today to speak to you.

"I guess none of you know what it's like to think that you're going to die when you're only fourteen years old. Well, I thought I was going to, because doctors said I didn't have much chance of surviving an operation. My second day in St. Michael's Hospital in Toronto, while I was lying in bed, getting ready for emergency surgery, a young nurse with a wonderful smile came to my bedside and spoke to me."

He stopped and looked at the crowd again, took a deep breath, and continued.

"This nurse took my hand and spoke to me in such a soft voice that I thought an angel had come down from heaven and that I was already dead. Her voice was so gentle that my fears were instantly calmed. I turned toward her and she started to sing. She sang for a few minutes, and then she talked to me of love, caring, and understanding. She made me forget all my worries.

"She told me stories of how, when she was a child in hospital, a wonderful nurse came to her when she was sick and sang to her. This showed what was needed by a young person who was frightened and worried. I thank God every day for that beautiful lady who sat by my side all night, whom I believe gave me the faith and strength to make it through that operation.

"You see, Mrs. Knight, I was in St. Michael's Children's Hospital in Toronto, Ontario, and the nurse I'm speaking of is Miss Jeanie Abbott. She told me so much about you that, when I heard they were giving a special tribute to you, I made this special trip to say thank you for taking Jeanie under your wing and letting her be my guardian angel."

With these words, Randy moved away from the podium to reveal Jeanie Abbott standing directly behind him. She blew a kiss to Sheila as they both walked toward each other, finally embracing. When they separated, Jeanie smiled at Sheila and spoke.

"Everything that I am today, as a nurse, I owe to you. I still treasure those talks we had when I was a little girl here at this hospital. My Christmas wouldn't have been complete without coming here to honour you tonight. You are indeed my Teddy Bear Lady."

Lucky's Discovery

by Lisa Ivany

Lucky Canning piled the last chunk of wood into her laden arms and kicked the shed door closed, making a shower of snow cascade from the roof. Her short auburn hair, tucked beneath a wool cap, avoided the avalanche, but a couple of wayward curls that hugged her temples were not so fortunate. Snow covered the ground on that mid-December morning and crunched under her feet as she walked to the front door of her cottage. It looked much better now with its new beige siding, windows, and shingled roof than it had back in May when she bought the place.

Constant reminders of her late husband, Morgan, had bombarded her at her home in Mount Pearl, and she had needed to get away to clear her head. When her friends, Melvin and Grace Wicks, had offered her the use of their cottage at Butt's Pond East for the Victoria Day weekend, she jumped at the opportunity. A retreat was just what she needed. Not only did it afford her the solace she needed to renew her spirit, but it also gave her the chance to polish her writing skills as a poet and short story writer. By the end of that weekend, she had fallen in love with the area, and bought a cabin at 34 Tulken Lane so she could have her own little piece of paradise.

With the help of her new community of neighbours at the pond, and especially Dave Lannigan, who had become more than just a friend since they met in May, her cottage was livable. Extensive renovations had transformed the stark cabin to a cozy cottage, and the final touch was the sign posted on the large birch tree in the centre of the drive, which said LUCKY'S LANDING. She painted the sign herself, adding a design of butterflies and also an inkwell to personalize it for the creative writer burning within her.

She obtained a four-month leave of absence from her job as assistant manager of the Battery Hotel in St. John's, and then had it extended to a year. Her supervisor was quite understanding of her need to get the cabin up to scratch, and appreciated how therapeutic this distraction was in helping her heart heal from Morgan's death. Although Dave was helping Lucky move on with her life, she still mourned the love she had shared with her late husband. She was thinking of him a lot lately, especially since his recent birthday. If not for his accident at sea, he would have turned thirty-three the previous week, less than a month before she turned the same age. If only his body had been recovered from the water's greedy clutches, then maybe she could have found some measure of closure.

The scent of cheese melting on the Italian pasta bake in the oven greeted Lucky on entering her cozy domain. She stacked the wood in the bin next to the Christmas tree and headed to the kitchen to finish preparing dinner before Dave arrived. He had been recently hired to teach English at a school in Botwood, which meant he only stayed at Butt's Pond on weekends. A month after Lucky moved to the Pond, Dave bought a cottage on the next road to be closer to her.

The delicious aroma from the oven caused her stomach to growl as she prepared a cheese loaf and tortellini Caesar salad to accompany it. She had been so busy working outside all day that she had completely forgotten to eat lunch, and couldn't wait for Dave to arrive so they could have dinner. She had prepared his favourite meal, which should put him in great spirits this evening. Not that he wasn't often in a good mood, because he was. It was just that, sometimes, when things weren't going the way he wanted, Dave revealed a different side of his personality, one that Lucky was uncomfortable with.

"Ahh!" she shrieked when she looked through her kitchen window. Movement had caught her eye, and she saw a tall, thin man wearing a black mask walking slowly across the deck. Her scream must have startled him as well, because he stopped in his tracks, turned, and ran. She pressed her face against the glass and watched him race toward the cover of trees encircling her property.

At that moment, Dave's van pulled into the driveway and Lucky ran outside with a new sense of bravado. She looked in the direction in which the mystery man had fled, but darkness had swallowed him whole. It had been easier to see him under the illumination of the coloured lights that lined the front patio. She leaned over the side railing, straining to see into the ebony forest, while Dave ascended the front steps.

"What are you looking at?" he asked.

"A man. Do you see him?"

"Yeah, I'm right here," he laughed.

"I'm serious, Dave. There was a man on my deck wearing a dark mask, and he ran that way." To emphasize her statement, she pointed toward the forest.

"Well, there's no one there now," he said. "Are you sure

you're not just conjuring him up from the pages of your manuscript?"

"I seriously doubt that, especially since I don't have a masked man in my current story."

She knew Dave was teasing her because she often became so immersed in her stories that she lost track of reality. More than once, when he had interrupted her while she wrote, she had called him by the name of one of her characters. Although she worked at the Battery, her true passion was writing and she hoped to one day be a published author.

"Something smells fantastic!" Dave said upon entering the cottage. "Is that your famous Italian pasta bake?"

"You have a good nose."

"You're the best."

He grabbed her in a bear hug and kissed her forehead before heading to the washroom to clean up. Lucky took that opportunity to close the blinds in the living room and kitchen, something she rarely did this early in the evening. Although she rationalized that perhaps the unexpected visitor was a figment of her imagination, it still sent a chill throughout her body.

She went to the guest bedroom and looked through the open slats of the mini-blind toward Tom Starkes's home next door. That was the direction in which the mystery man had run. The large pole light at the back of Tom's place was on, and it lit up the entire grounds, but there was nothing there. Lucky wondered if the stranger was just outside the periphery of the light and was spying on her cottage at this moment. Goosebumps formed along her arms at the thought of being watched, and she quickly shut the blind.

During dinner, Dave was very attentive, and complimentary of Lucky's culinary skills. Afterward, he cuddled with her on the sofa through two movies. However, when she asked him to stay in the guest bedroom for the night, he blew a gasket.

"Lucky, when are you going to stop tiptoeing around this relationship and let me spend the night in *your* room?"

"You know I'm not ready for that yet. You said you understood."

"I did at first, but it's time for you to move on with your life . . . with me. You've never asked me to spend the night before, and now that you do, it's to stay in the guest room! Why is that?"

"The stranger on my patio spooked me a little, that's all," she said timidly. "Just forget about it."

Frustrated, he picked up his reading glasses from the table and flung them across the room; they crashed against the wall. Lucky had never seen him display such aggressive behaviour and hoped it would not escalate.

"Do you think I'm a eunuch?" he asked. "I have needs like any other man, and I think I've been patient long enough."

He grabbed her roughly by the forearms and yanked her into his embrace. He slipped one arm behind her to gain a better grip and used the other hand to pull her face closer. His mouth came down hard upon hers as he tried to extract a kiss, but she resisted, pushing against him.

"Dave, stop it!" she screamed.

"I haven't even started."

"You're hurting me."

"Then stop fighting me, honey."

"This is the last straw, Dave. I want you to leave this instant and don't ever come back."

"Lucky, stop playing hard to get. You know you want this as much as I do."

He pulled her toward the bedroom with difficulty, as she was kicking and screaming the whole way. However, her strength was no match for his and he quickly had her pinned to the bed. She continued to scream and fight with as much strength as she could muster, but it was not enough to dislodge him.

Suddenly, there was no weight on her. His body was jerked completely into the air and he was pushed out of her room. There was a scuffle in the hallway and she sprang to the doorway just as Dave's upper body hit the floor. The masked man had him pinned, and only released him when he promised to leave without further trouble.

The stranger held Dave's arm behind his back in a tight grip as he pushed him through the front door and escorted him to his vehicle. As Dave backed out of the driveway, Lucky's rescuer stood rooted to the spot and watched the van until it reached the end of Tulken Lane and the tail lights were no longer visible. He then returned to the deck, where Lucky was standing in the doorway.

"Are you okay, ma'am?" he asked.

"Yes, I'm fine."

"Good night, then."

Before she could thank him, he had vanished into the night, as quickly and quietly as if he had been a ghost.

* * *

Lucky was drying dishes from breakfast when she heard footsteps on the stairs of her patio, followed by rapping at the door. She brushed her apprehension aside and opened the door, expecting to see Dave, but it was Tom Starkes from next door, accompanied by Harvey Pike from across the road.

"Good morning, gentlemen," she greeted. "Come in."

"Sorry to bother you so early, Lucky, but we just heard about the trouble you had last night. Are you okay?" Harvey asked.

"Yes, I'm fine, now that Dave and I have split."

"Are you sure everything's okay?" Tom asked. "From what Chase tells me, you were in serious trouble last night."

"Who's Chase?" she asked.

"He's our new handyman, and the one who came to your aid," Tom answered. "I actually sent him over earlier in the evening to see if you needed any chores done. Didn't he introduce himself?"

"He didn't get the chance. When I saw a strange man in a mask outside my window, I screamed and he ran away. I think I scared him more than he scared me."

"He may look a little spooky in that mask, but I assure you he's harmless, and quite a good worker, too."

"Yes, he cleared some trees for me yesterday and did a great job," Harvey added. "I think he'd be good protection for you, too."

"Thanks, but I don't need protection from Dave. I made it pretty clear to him last night to stay away."

"Okay," Tom said. "If you say so, but don't hesitate to call if you need us."

After Lucky reassured her neighbours that everything was fine, she donned her jacket and gloves and went to the woodshed. After the large truckload of firewood she received yesterday, she knew she had a full day's work ahead of her to get it stacked neatly inside.

When she arrived at the back of the cottage, her jaw dropped in astonishment. The huge pile of wood was gone! She didn't know what to think; surely no one could have taken it, especially without being seen. She raced to the shed to see if anything else was missing, since she knew she had left the door unlocked the previous evening. Extending the entire length of the shed, and halfway across the floor, was row upon row of neatly stacked firewood, at a comfortable height for Lucky to reach the top row.

Perplexed, she wondered who would have done such a gracious act. It certainly wasn't Dave, because he hadn't arrived until dinnertime, and had spent the rest of the evening inside with her before he went storming off. By that time, he was certainly in no frame of mind to do her any favours. Whoever was responsible, she was grateful, because it would have taken her the entire day to stack the wood, preventing her from going to Gander to pick up the last of the Christmas presents on her list.

Her red Toyota Corolla turned west onto the Trans-Canada Highway. The light snowfall only required her intermittent wipers. She turned on the radio, and daggers of pain shot through her heart when she heard Garth Brooks's familiar rendition of "The Gift." It had been Morgan's favourite carol, and one she could no longer bear to hear. The previous Christmas he had played the song so often, she had joked that Garth was getting laryngitis. They had been ecstatically happy, thinking they would spend many Christmases together, not knowing how soon their plans and dreams would come to an end.

She turned off the radio and wiped away her tears. *Pull yourself together, girl*, she silently admonished. She shook her head as if to clear it of Morgan's image, but she knew it was in vain, because he had been permanently etched in her mind since the day they had met. It was on her thirtieth birthday, and her friends and co-workers from the Battery Hotel had thrown a surprise party for her. Morgan came to the party with a friend, and it was love at first sight. A year later he proposed, and seven months after that they were married and looking forward to a blissfully happy future. How quickly things could change.

She pulled into the Wal-Mart parking lot in Gander just as she made a pact with herself to stop comparing other men to Morgan. Sure, Dave had shown his true nature and she was glad to be rid of him, but she also knew in her heart that it would be nearly impossible to find a man to measure up to her late husband. Perhaps that was the whole problem. Morgan was a true gentleman who put her needs before his own, opening car doors for her, giving her his jacket when she was chilled, massaging her neck after hours at the keyboard, and so on. She just had to realize that not all men were that attentive, but there had to be others out there somewhere with other good qualities.

* * *

By the time Lucky returned to her cottage, a moderate amount of snow had fallen and she was sure she would have to get out her shovel, but then she received her second surprise of the day. Her driveway had been cleared, right up to her door. The sound of a shovel repetitively lifting and throwing snow greeted her ears as she walked around the side of her home. Chase had his back to her as he shovelled a walkway to her shed, and so engrossed in his task he had not heard her approach.

"Hi there," she said.

Startled, he visibly jumped before turning around to face her. Instead of answering, he waved his hand in acknowledgment of her greeting.

"I didn't mean to scare you," she smiled.

"That's okay."

"Thanks so much for clearing my driveway," she said. "How much do I owe you?"

"Nothing."

"I don't expect you to do all this work and not get paid," she insisted.

"My pleasure."

Lucky was baffled that a complete stranger would be so kind. It was a lot of hard work to shovel her long driveway, and now he was making a pathway for her to get to the shed. A thought struck her.

"Did you stack my firewood yesterday?"

Without answering, he nodded his head.

"Wow! That was an enormous task. You must let me pay you for that."

"No need," he responded.

Lucky realized Chase was a man of few words, probably due to intense shyness, but he certainly had a big heart. She wanted to repay him for his kindness, but he didn't want to take her money. Since her greatest passion next to writing was cooking, it was easy to come up with a satisfactory solution.

"Dinner is at six o'clock and I'd like you to join me," she said.

When it looked as if he was about to object, Lucky stated, "I don't like eating alone, so I won't take no for an answer."

The interior of the cottage was soon filled with the sound of Christmas music. She sang along with a smile on her face, which she attributed to the fact that she would not be walking on eggshells around Dave any longer. Instead of feeling depressed after their breakup, she felt better than she had for quite a while and was looking forward to sharing a meal with her guardian angel. She was just taking the cranberry pot roast from the oven when she heard a tap on the front door.

"Come in. You're just in time," she said as Chase entered.

He placed a bottle of wine on the table and asked, "Can I help?"

"Actually, you can uncork that bottle you just brought and pour us a drink. The wine glasses and corkscrew are on the counter."

By the time Lucky had placed the meat on the table, along with the roasted vegetables and stuffing, Chase had finished his task. He removed his jacket and waited for her to sit before taking the opposite seat. His long-sleeved white cotton shirt was tucked inside his denims and his black mask had been replaced with a white one. It enclosed his entire head so that Lucky could not even decipher the colour of his hair. He was tall and slim with soft hazel eyes.

"It's delicious," he commented upon tasting the meal.

"Thank you."

They ate in silence a moment when she asked, "Why don't you take off your mask?"

"I never take it off."

"Why not?"

"Car accident," he said. "Ruined my face."

"It must be stifling. Do you ever take it off?"

"Only when I'm alone."

"I don't mind if you remove it," she persisted. "I'm sure you'd be more comfortable."

"No thanks."

Lucky realized he was too self-conscious to do as she asked and dropped the matter. She hoped he would eventually let down his guard and trust her as much as she had already come to trust him.

* * *

Christmas Day and Boxing Day came and went without any further contact from Dave, and Lucky was able to breathe easier. She was told by a neighbour that he was talking about selling his cottage in the new year and leaving Butt's Pond for good. Dave had a lot of pride, and being ousted from his girlfriend's home by another man must have been humiliating. Enough to keep him away, and that was fine with Lucky. Of course, the new deadbolt that Chase had purchased and installed as part of her Christmas gift ensured her safety.

December 27 was Lucky's birthday, and Chase came by to cook dinner. Afterward, he extracted a small gift-wrapped box from his shirt pocket and handed it to her.

"Happy birthday," he said.

"You didn't have to get me anything," she said. "Cooking dinner was a gift in itself."

"You deserve much more."

She unwrapped her present and beamed when she saw the round opal, held by four golden prongs, hanging from a gold chain.

"It's beautiful," she sighed. "I love it."

She wrapped her arms around his neck and squeezed tightly until he hugged her in return. She pulled back and kissed his lips before saying, "Thank you." Instead of leaving his embrace, something compelled her to look into his eyes, and that's when she was caught in his hypnotic stare. She slid her hands up his chest and around to the back of his neck, gently gliding his head down toward hers. He needed no further persuasion; his mouth claimed hers in a hungry kiss. Her lips were soon parted, allowing the entrance of his gentle tongue, and she welcomed the long-suppressed passion that now coursed through her body.

Love's remembered kiss flooded through Lucky's consciousness as she recalled the last time Morgan had kissed her like this. Actually, it was exactly like this!

She broke off the kiss, and before Chase knew what was happening, she had grabbed the mask and pulled it completely free from his head.

"Oh my God!" she exclaimed. "Morgan! Is it really you?"

He nodded in answer.

"How can this be? You died."

"It would have been better if I had."

"How can you say such a thing?" she asked incredulously.

"Lucky, take a look at my face, or at least what's left of it."

"All I see is the man I fell in love with."

To anyone else, the large red scars covering the left side of Morgan's face would be hard to ignore, but Lucky was blind to them. She was looking at him through the eyes of her heart and saw only a Christmas miracle that had brought her soulmate back from the dead.

* * *

Morgan told Lucky how he was on his way to the engine room when an explosion sent him flying over the railing and out into the ocean. He was fortunate to have found a piece of wreckage to crawl up on before losing consciousness. When he came to, he was under the care of two Norwegian brothers on their small fishing vessel.

Once Morgan had taken a look at himself in the mirror, he refused to return to Newfoundland. He didn't want his wife to be saddled with an ogre, and it would tear his heart out to see her look at him with revulsion or even pity every day for the rest of their lives. The brothers tried to convince him to let his family know he was alive, but Morgan knew Lucky would never leave him, because of her sense of duty. He couldn't live with her under those terms.

"So, why did you come back now?" Lucky asked when he had finished his story.

"I couldn't stay away any longer, not knowing how you were. I needed to see for myself that you were okay, and then I was going to walk away," he said. "When I saw the trouble you were in with that creep, Dave, I had to stick around. Then it was becoming harder and harder to leave you."

"I'm glad you stayed." Her eyes misted when she said, "Promise me you'll never leave me again."

"What about the scars?"

"I don't see any."

"Then, I promise to stay."

Lucky had begun her thirty-third birthday with her new friend, Chase, and ended it in the arms of her husband, Morgan. What a perfect birthday gift, to discover she had fallen in love, twice, with the same man.

CHRISTMAS TRIVIA

Different Ways to Say "Merry Christmas"

Afrikaans: Geseënde Kersfees
African: Rehus-Beal-Ledeats
Albanian: Gezur Krislinjden
Arabic: Idah Saidan Wa Sanah Jadidah
Argentine: Feliz Navidad
Bohemian: Vesele Vanoce
Brazilian: Boas Festas e Feliz Ano Novo
Chilean: Feliz Navidad
Chinese (Cantonese): Gun Tso Sun Tan'Gung Haw Sun
Chinese (Mandarin): Kung His Hsin Nien bing Chu Shen Tan
Cornish: Nadelik looan na looan blethen noweth
Croatian: Sretan Bozic
Czech: Prejeme Vam Vesele Vanoce a stastny Novy Rok
Danish: Glædelig Jul
Dutch: Vrolijk Kerstfeest en een Gelukkig Nieuwjaari
    or Zalig Kerstfeast
English: Merry Christmas
Finnish: Hyvaa joulua
French: Joyeux Noel
Gaelic: Nollaig chridheil agus Bliadhna mhath ùr
German: Weihnachten
Greek: Kala Christouyenna

Hawaiian: Mele Kalikimaka

Hebrew: Mo'adim Lesimkha. Chena tova

Hindi: Shub Naya Baras

Hungarian: Kellemes Karacsonyi unnepeket

Icelandic: Gledileg Jol

Indonesian: Selamat Hari Natal

Iraqi: Idah Saidan Wa Sanah Jadidah

Irish: Nollaig shona dhuit or Nodlaig mhaith chugnat

Italian: Buone Feste Natalizie

Japanese: Shinnen omedeto. Kurisumasu omedeto

Korean: Sung Tan Chuk Ha

Latin: Natale hilare et Annum Faustum

Macedonian: Sreken Bozhik

Maori: Meri Kirihimete

Navajo: Merry Keshmish

Norwegian: God Jul or Gledelig Jul

Polish: Wesolych Swiat Bozego Narodzenia or Boze Narodz

Portugese: Feliz Natal

Rumanian: Sarbatori vesele

Russian: Pozdrevlyayu s prazdnikom Rozhdestva is Novim

Serbian: Hristos se rodi

Spanish: Feliz Navidad

Swedish: God Jul and (Och) Ett Gott Nytt År

Turkish: Noeliniz Ve Yeni Yiliniz Kutlu Olsun

Ukranian: Srozhdestvom Kristovym

Vietnamese: Chung Mung Giang Sinh

Welsh: Nadolig Llawen

Yugoslavian: Cestitamo Bozic

Darkness

by Robert Hunt

December 21, 1973

Being without full sight was nothing new to Matthew Lush. His uncommon sense of feeling and touch were magnified twofold when trying to correct his sense of direction and equilibrium. Though he was not legally blind, he had lost all but twenty-five percent of his vision many years ago, and sometimes his perception of things made it very hard to distinguish one object from another. Matt still had nightmares of the accident that had robbed him of his sight in 1953. Many times he recalled that day and how, as a six-year-old, he had taken that dare from his friends to climb on top of his home and walk along its roof. Whatever had compelled him to do it was still not clear in his mind, but the fall certainly was. He remembered the bruises, the broken arm, and the vision loss he had suffered when he struck his head on the tree as he fell. Though his injuries were not life-threatening and he healed quickly, his sight had not returned in full.

These thoughts flashed back into Matt's mind as he rode the back trails behind his cabin on the Salmonier Line in Holyrood, twenty years later. Matt was always fascinated by the outdoors and loved the peace and quiet it afforded him. Skidooing, though it was with limited vision, offered him an escape and freedom from his everyday concerns. He was immersed in and in tune with nature when he was outside. He knew every trail and river within miles of his cabin in any direction. Out here, his enhanced sense of smell, touch, and hearing were all he needed.

Christmas Eve was just three days away, and Matt was looking forward to the arrival of his parents. They would stay with him at the cabin until Boxing Day, when they would leave to visit his brother's wife's family in Embree. Although Matt enjoyed his parents' company, he was also quite content to be on his own in the wilderness.

Matt navigated his Ski-Doo around Hollow Pond and onto Baker's Road. It had started to snow lightly and was becoming dark as he descended the hill toward the pond. Off in the distance a loon cried, sending the sharp message that all was well with him. As Matt entered a hairpin turn at the start of the pond, he heard a small shout echo in the forest.

Instinctively, he turned his head to determine the location of the noise. It was muffled, and seemed to be coming from somewhere in the distance to his right.

He stopped his Ski-Doo at the edge of the pond, shut off the engine, and listened. Matt wasn't sure if it was just his imagination or not. He got off his snowmobile, walked a short distance, and again listened for the sound. Sure enough, the shout came again. He walked back along the trail, started the Ski-Doo, and headed toward the voice. As he rounded a sharp turn and manoeuvred the vehicle parallel to Hollow Pond, the noise grew louder.

"Help, please, someone help me!" a voice screamed hysterically.

Matt gunned the powerful machine for another few hundred yards toward the head of the pond. He stopped and scanned the pond before he let his instincts take over. Approximately two hundred feet from shore, a young boy was calling frantically.

"Please, help me. I can't hang on much longer!"

Matt immediately jumped off the Ski-Doo and looked out over the ice. Obviously, the young man had fallen through as he attempted to cross Hollow Pond. *There's no time to lose,* Matt thought as he ran back to his machine, opened his backpack, and took out a three-hundred-foot rope. He secured a double-looped knot around the nearest tree and headed toward the boy. Making another loop knot, he raced to the spot where the boy had fallen through. Examining the water, he saw no outline of a snowmobile or trike and guessed that the water here was very deep; he concluded that the boy's vehicle had sunk to the bottom.

"Don't kick around in the water. Try to remain still," Matt yelled. "I'm coming to get you!"

The young man tried to remain calm, but fear took over as his snowsuit grew heavy with water. Matt lay flat on the ice and started to crawl to the frightened youth. It was only a matter of time before the thin slab of ice that supported the boy broke free, taking them both under. Within seconds, Matt reached him. Suddenly, the ice cracked with a thunderous report and the boy started to sink. Matt knew he had no time to spare. He was wearing an insulated snowsuit and knew that he could survive the cold water for more than a few minutes, whereas the young man couldn't. Without hesitation, he stood up and moved to the opening in the ice and dove in headfirst. The severe cold hit him as he searched frantically for the youth.

He noticed the boy's glove in the murky water. Matt ignored the bitter cold, and made a desperate effort to grab the boy's arm. His hand lunged out, and though he missed the young man's hand, he did manage to secure his jacket. With tremendous effort, Matt looped the rope around the boy's torso and secured it tightly. With a quick push up from the bottom, he propelled himself and the boy to the surface. They burst out of the water, gasping for air. Matt looked at the young man and was relieved to see that he was breathing.

Though nearly frozen, Matt quickly pushed the boy upward onto the ice. He shouted, "Grab the rope, son, and start pulling yourself to the shore!"

Though starting to panic, the boy understood what Matt was saying to him and grabbed the rope with his frozen gloves. Bit by bit, he slowly pulled himself to the shore. After what seemed an eternity, the young man reached the shore as the lights of several snowmobiles approached the pond.

With the young man out of the water, Matt tried to push himself onto the ice, but something was terribly wrong. He tried to move, but his body would not respond. It seemed as if his lower body was not there. The rope had been thrown back to him, but as Matt tried to pull it closer, his hands would not heed his efforts.

A strange feeling of comfort came over him, and he felt a great warmth that he had never known before. He looked at the sky and saw a brilliant light descend, and he felt fully at peace. Suddenly, he could see what he had never seen before. All the stars were shining brightly at him as the cold enveloped him. The last thing he saw as he glanced at the shore was the young man pulling himself up on the pond's edge. He closed his eyes and let himself slip below the surface and into the darkness.

* * *

December 21, 2003

Reuben Hiscock slowly drove around Hollow Pond in his pickup truck. He looked at his wife, Susan, and smiled. He stared into the rear-view mirror at his ten-year-old son, Jeremy, sitting in the back seat looking out the window. All were silent as they approached the edge of the pond. They exited the truck upon arrival. Reuben looked at his wife and son, then at the flower he was holding in his hand, and led them out to the centre of the pond, where he proceeded to cut a hole in the ice with his auger. He placed the flower on top of the water. A tear rolled down Reuben's cheek as he held his wife's and child's hands.

He looked at Susan and whispered to her, "Greater love hath no man than this, that he lay down his life for his friends."

Turning to his son, Reuben said, "Jeremy, I want you to touch this water. Feel it in your hand, and remember, with me and your mom, what happened here thirty years ago."

With cupped hands, he offered some of the water to his son. Jeremy pressed his hand between his father's and smiled at him.

"You see, son, I've been coming here every year on this date since you were born, and I want you to pay tribute to a man who gave his life so that your daddy could have his. I was a little older than you when this happened, one winter a long time ago. I took a Ski-Doo, against my father's wishes, and tried to cross this pond, but fell through the ice. Because of the bravery of a near-blind man, I'm alive today."

Reuben looked at his wife and saw tears in her eyes. He sat his son down on a small rock nearby and continued. "I can still remember the chill of the water, the coldness that surrounded me, and the peace I felt when I thought I was going to die. But as I was about to slip away from this earth, a strong arm came out of nowhere and took my shoulder. It seemed that God Himself had other plans for me that night."

Reuben stopped speaking and stared out over Hollow Pond and the past.

"Because of a man called Matthew Lush, your daddy is here with you. I never want you to forget him or what he did for me that night. I want you to promise me, if I am not with you, to come here every year at Christmas, on December 21, with your own children and lay a flower in Hollow Pond to show respect for this man. Will you do that for me, son?"

Jeremy smiled and nodded. "I will, Daddy. I promise."

Reuben hugged his son and wife and led them back to the truck. He turned once more, waved, and said, "Thank you, Mr. Lush, for the gift of life. God bless you."

As he said this, Reuben saw the flower move along the top of the water. It made one revolution, then slowly sank to the bottom of the pond.

CHRISTMAS TRIVIA

Christmas Traditions of the World

Indian Christmas

In India, Christians decorate mango and banana trees during Christmas and sometimes adorn their houses with mango leaves. Some have clay oil lamps for decorations, which are lit and placed on roofs and walls.

On Christmas Eve, churches are filled with poinsettias, and candles are lit for the evening service.

Japanese Christmas

In Japan, Christmas is celebrated much the same way as in Western cultures. People exchange presents and eat a turkey dinner on Christmas Day in houses decorated with mistletoe and evergreens. It is not uncommon to hear families joyously singing Christmas carols.

The Japanese version of Santa Claus is a priest who appears as a kind old man carrying a huge sack. He is believed to have eyes in the back of his head, so children must behave when he is near.

The most important day of the year in the Japanese culture is New Year's Day. The houses are cleaned thoroughly and families dress in their best clothes. The father is followed through the home as he throws dried beans in the corners of the rooms to drive out evil spirits and bring in good fortune.

Italian Christmas

Italians claim the origin of the nativity scene, and it is one of their most treasured symbols of the holiday. St. Francis of Assisi asked a man in the village of Greccio to create a manger scene. A Mass was performed in front of this early nativity scene, and it has been a central part of the Italian heritage ever since.

The exchanging of presents takes place on January 6, which is called the Feast of the Epiphany, and honours the visit to the Christ child by the Magi. Children are visited by La Befana, who gives gifts to the good and punishes the bad.

Young Samaritan

by Lisa Ivany

Muriel Collins entered her daughter's home in Hare Bay to babysit her five-year-old grandson, Joey, while his parents went out to a Christmas dinner with some friends. She followed Joey's voice to the family room at the back of the house where he sat by the tree, singing carols along with a CD he was playing.

When Joey saw her enter, he ran to her and exclaimed, "Grandma! You're finally here!" He wrapped his little arms around her and stood on tiptoes to give her a big kiss.

"Well, that's a wonderful greeting, little man," she said as she laid aside the shopping bag she was carrying, and lowered herself into his embrace.

"Guess what!"

"What?" she answered while seating herself on the sofa.

He held up a toy in his hand and said, "I finally saved up enough money to buy this Dynoman action figure I've been wanting for so long!"

"But Joey, Christmas will soon be here and perhaps Santa was planning on bringing it to you.

"That's what Mom said, but I forgot to mail my letter to Santa, so he probably doesn't know what I want."

Then a voice from the doorway said, "Hi, Mom. I didn't know you were here." Samantha bustled into the room with a red-and-green shoebox and handed it to her mother while buttoning up her jacket. She said, "Did you remember to bring your items for the shoebox?"

"Yes, I think I have everything on my list. Did you manage to get everything on yours?"

"I think so, but you can double-check when I leave. I have everything placed on the kitchen table," Samantha said. "Jack probably has the car warmed up by now, so I better get going." She looked at Joey and said, "You be a good boy for Grandma while we're gone, okay?

"I will, Mom."

Muriel retrieved her package and went to the kitchen where she emptied it onto the table, along with the articles Samantha had purchased. She went through the list to make sure they had everything they needed, then started preparing the shoebox. There was an array of school supplies, toiletries, candy, and a couple of small toys to be arranged in the box.

With his curiosity aroused, Joey asked, "Grandma, why are you filling up that shoebox?"

"Well, Joey, this is a special shoebox that's going to be shipped overseas to a boy about your age in a different part of the world who would otherwise have no Christmas presents. Many people in our country fill these shoeboxes each Christmas for a little boy or girl who basically has nothing."

"Why not, Grandma?"

"They live in countries where there is very little food or clothing for some people, and many of them have no mommy or daddy to care for them. There are far too many kids who have none of these things, and also have no home, so they wander the streets. This box is just a little gesture of goodwill on our part to help give the children a nice Christmas and to let them know that there are people in the world who care about them."

Joey grimaced. "Why are you putting soap and combs in the box? No kid is gonna want that for Christmas!"

Muriel smiled at the innocence of her young grandson, thankful he had never had to experience a life of poverty like the recipient of this box.

She said, "The little boy who receives this box will enjoy everything in it, including the soap and combs. These items are actually considered a luxury over there. Don't worry. As you can see, your mom and I have also included some candy and toys."

Satisfied with her answer, Joey left the kitchen and Muriel continued with her task. A few minutes later, Joey returned with his action figure and passed it to his grandmother. He said, "Here, Grandma. Do you think the little boy who gets this box would like my Dynoman?"

"I'm sure he would, Joey, but you have saved up a long time to buy that toy. There is no need for you to part with it. Besides, your mom and I have plenty to go in the box."

"Please, Grandma, I really want this to go to someone who will have fun with it. I have lots of toys and I'll be getting more at Christmas anyway."

Muriel was impressed with her grandson's generosity and accepted his gift. She squeezed it down into the box in the space that was left. "A perfect fit," she said as she placed the lid on the box.

When Samantha and Jack returned home, Joey was

asleep in bed. Muriel told them what had transpired that evening and what a true Samaritan they were raising.

* * *

Christmas morning, Joey excitedly opened his presents. He had a new sense of appreciation for everything he received as he thought about the boys and girls in other countries who had so little. He wondered if they were at this same moment opening up their green-and-red shoeboxes.

After he finished opening all of his gifts, his mother said, "There's one more present behind the tree. Why don't you see who it's for?"

On his hands and knees, Joey extended his arm to the back of the tree and grasped the brightly coloured package. He backed out and said, "It's for me from Santa." He opened up the package and couldn't believe his eyes as he held a Dynoman action figure. "Wow!" he exclaimed. "Santa *did* know what I wanted for Christmas after all."

For the rest of the day he played with the various toys and games he received that morning, and wherever he went, his Dynoman accompanied him. He asked his mother that evening at the dinner table, "Mom, do you think the boy who received our shoebox likes his Dynoman as much as I like mine?"

Samantha answered, "I'm sure he does, Joey. I think it's a safe bet to say that you helped make his Christmas a lot brighter."

Poor Bill

by Robert Hunt

Janet Spencer did not believe in angels, at least not until she met Norman Patterson. She always believed that no such thing as angels existed, until one actually came to her rescue, or, more precisely, to the rescue of a family member. It helped her realize that, for every person in this world who is cruel and vindictive to others, there is another who is good and kind. Today, Janet sits with friends on Christmas Eve and tells them what happened years ago, on the day she started to believe in angels.

* * *

A week before Christmas, Janet was observing a homeless man from her office window. She worked as a lawyer with Stacey, Kearns and Young. Janet's office overlooked the business district of Corner Brook. Sometimes, when her day became too hectic, or she was not attending court and needed a moment of peace, she would take a break from her paperwork and look out through her window at the many people who walked up and down the sidewalks. She wondered what kind of lives they lived as they bustled to and from work, or rushed along the busy street getting ready for Christmas. She wondered how much heartache and happiness they had in their daily lives, where and what they were rushing to.

For a long time now, Janet had noticed one man in particular sitting peacefully next to the coffee shop talking to passersby, glancing in his tin cup while he waited for people to drop money into it. She guessed the money he collected was for food, as she had never seen him drink. Many times she had seen him sitting there just staring into space or reading a book, and she had often wondered what his story was. Everyone had a story to tell. She found out that people had nicknamed him "Poor Bill," but she knew very little else about him, except that he seemed to observe things as he sat there, and that he was an avid reader.

On this particular day, as Janet looked across the street from her second-storey window, he produced a book and started to read. She was curious about the cover; she couldn't see the book's name but it looked familiar. For about ten minutes she tried to make out the title of the book. Finally, frustrated, she pressed on the intercom button and spoke to her secretary.

"Paula, do we have a pair of binoculars here some-where? I remember we had them here last year when we went on that hiking trip."

Janet nodded at Paula's response and went to the filing cabinet where the secretary had told her they might be. She returned to her chair, and within a few seconds had focused on the book that Poor Bill held in his hands. She was amazed when she saw the name: *A Tale of Two*

Cities, by Charles Dickens. Strange, Janet thought. Why would a homeless person be reading that kind of a book?

As she worked through the day, she grew more curious as to why a transient would read such a book. What benefits could he get out of reading something that might be beyond his scope of understanding? Surely only an educated man would be reading such a book as *A Tale of Two Cities*. It was none of her business, she knew, but she would make a point of asking him when she spoke to him as she passed his way tomorrow.

* * *

The next day, when Janet went to work, she walked across the street as if to enter the small coffee shop situated directly across from her office. She had been thinking about what she would ask Poor Bill. Reaching the shop, she lingered close to him, looking into the shop window as if deciding what she would have to eat. Bill looked up over his reading glasses as Janet watched him from the corner of her eye. She didn't know how to approach a homeless person, let alone ask him the foolish question that had been in her mind since yesterday. Poor Bill broke the silence.

"Good morning, Miss Spencer, and how are we today?"

Janet stared at him, wide-eyed.

"I'm sorry, but how do you know my name?"

"I know almost everyone's name around this area. For one, I've seen you, among others, going in and out of Stacey, Kearns and Young's offices across the street. Since you carry a briefcase, I'm guessing that you're a lawyer, but since I haven't seen your name on the front door where you work, I'm guessing you haven't been made a full partner yet. I'm also guessing that this is your ambition." He smiled and continued. "As for your name, you do have it engraved on your case."

Janet smiled back and said, "You're very observant, Mr. Bill."

Poor Bill looked at Janet with a "Next question?" kind of look. Janet felt a little embarrassed. Again, Bill broke the silence.

"You have another question for me, do you not?"

Now Janet felt foolish and didn't know how to go about asking him.

Bill sensed this and said, very quietly, "Please, don't be shy. I've been asked many questions by many people as I sit here from day to day, and I'm always willing to answer them if I can."

Feeling more at ease, Janet blurted out, before realizing how it would sound, "I'm sorry, Mr. Bill, but I saw you reading *A Tale of Two Cities*, and I wondered why you should read such a –" She searched for the right word. "–delicate book."

Poor Bill just smiled his pleasant smile again and replied to her in a calm tone. "As you can see, Miss Spencer, I don't have much to do in my line of work, so I sit here and observe life, and when I become tired of that, I read a little. Over the past few days I just felt compelled to read *A Tale of Two Cities*. It's been a long time since I've read it."

Janet sensed that this man had come from a different background than your average street person. She hoped she hadn't offended him and knew that to save herself any more embarrassment she would have to leave in the next few seconds. She thanked him for the conversation and said, "I hope you don't think that I was prying. I was just curious. Thanks so much for your time, Mr. Bill. I should be getting back to work."

"You're quite welcome, Miss Spencer. Come chat again sometime."

Janet started to walk across the street when Poor Bill spoke up again.

"By the way, Miss Spencer, my name is not Poor Bill. It's really Norman Patterson, and you can call me Norm."

Janet acknowledged his comment and replied, "You can call me Janet."

* * *

In the months that followed, Janet spoke to Norman Patterson many times as she walked to work, and slowly he revealed his life story. His charm, charisma, and intelligence showed that he was a very well-educated person. One day, Janet asked him if he cared to come inside the coffee shop and have lunch with her. He agreed to do so, but only if she allowed him to pay. She accepted, and Norman Patterson's full story finally came out.

Norman had been born in Winnipeg, Manitoba, to a family of six children, three boys and three girls. He was fifty-five years old. He had dropped out of school in grade nine to help his older sister support the family, after their father had left them and their mother to fend for themselves. Norman had taken a job with McCormack Oil, working his way up the corporate ladder to become vice-president of sales in one of its subsidiary companies. He went to night school and then on to the University of Manitoba when he was thirty-six years old to earn his geology degree.

He continued to work his way up, and was soon married with two children, a boy and a girl. However, devoting all of his energies to his job eventually led to the breakup of his marriage and the loss of his children's admiration. Norman immersed himself in his job and further neglected and alienated his family and most of his friends. He finally took notice of the rift that had grown between him and his children, but it wasn't until his twenty-two-year-old son committed suicide that he realized life was more important than money, so he gave up everything he owned and decided to live on the streets. After Glen's death, which Norman felt he had caused, he couldn't bear to talk to his ex-wife and daughter, as they also seemed to blame him, and he left to travel across Canada. That was seven years ago, and he hadn't contacted or heard from them since.

Janet came to realize how lucky she was. She had been happily married to her husband, Don, for ten years, and they had a beautiful eight-year-old daughter, Melissa, who was the love of their lives. How tragic life is for some people, Janet thought, as she listened to Norman. She felt compassion for this man and wondered before lunch ended if he would be interested in working for her.

"Norm, my husband and I have a large farm on the outskirts of Corner Brook, which we find very hard to maintain. We were thinking of hiring someone to care for the grounds. If you're interested, we would like to hire you to take care of it for us."

"Thank you for the offer, Janet, but I'm not sure. I'd feel that I would be intruding on you and your family, and what would your husband say when he found out that you were thinking of hiring a street person?"

"I've already told him about you, and he's looking forward to meeting you. Please think about it and let me know."

"I'll give it some thought," was all Norman would say.

* * *

Norman eventually took the job and soon began a friendship with Janet and Don that gave him back the sense of self-worth he needed in his life. Janet needed to feel that her decision to hire Norman had been the right thing to do, and soon admiration and trust developed between them. For months, Norman took care of the grounds and grew very close to the family. Melissa was the make-believe granddaughter that Norman wished he could have had. She was charming, well-mannered, and mature for her age.

Life changed for Norman, and soon he settled into a degree of contentment he had not enjoyed for seven years. He did his work with a vigour and sincerity that made Janet and Don trust him implicitly. When they travelled for pleasure, or had work-related business away from the city and, at times, outside the province, Norman took care of their property. Melissa stayed with her grandmother in Pasadena, but sometimes they came to visit him while he cared for the farm.

It was on one such occasion that life caused another change for Norman Patterson and his new-found friends. Don, as a manager for the provincial government's water-works department, was in Gander and Janet was on business in Calgary, when Janet's mother, June, and Melissa came to visit the farm. Norman took a break from his duties to take them out on a hayride aboard a horse-drawn cart. Later that day, June and Melissa decided to take a swim in the indoor pool while Norman tended to his chores. The sun was starting to dip beneath the mountains when a sharp cry echoed from the back of the house.

Norman ran toward the scream. As he rounded the corner of the house, he collided with a terrified Melissa. Norman held her by the shoulders, speaking quietly to calm her down.

"Melissa, slow down. Take a deep breath and tell me what's happening."

Melissa was wide-eyed with terror. She looked at Norman and started to speak. Nothing came out. She pointed toward the corner of the house. Norman sat her down on the patio chair and told her to stay put. He rushed around the corner of the house and looked at the indoor pool. Sixty-two-year-old June Simmons lay floating face down in the water. She was not moving. Quickly, Norman raced inside, pulling off his shoes as he ran, and plunged into the warm water. He swiftly turned June over to check for a pulse. It was beating very slowly. He knew that time was of the essence. Looping his hand under her chin and drawing her to the side of the pool, Norman pushed her up onto the concrete deck, easing his hand under her head for support.

After checking the woman's pulse, he started to apply CPR. A few minutes later, June Simmons was still unresponsive. Norman knew that he could only administer CPR for a short time. Then he remembered Melissa.

"Melissa, I need your help! Your nanny is having trouble breathing. You have to come and help me."

Melissa came inside and looked up at him in shock after she noticed her grandmother on the concrete. The little girl seemed too afraid to move. She took several tentative steps in Norman's direction.

"Melissa, look at me. This is not your fault. You have to go down the road to Mr. Butler's farm. Tell him your nanny is having trouble and to call an ambulance. Do you understand what I am saying to you?"

All too glad to have been given an excuse to get out of there, Melissa nodded, bolted outside, and raced away to the Butler farmhouse.

Norman turned back to June and again started CPR. He applied the few resuscitative techniques he knew and was relieved when June's pulse began to increase. Letting out a sigh of relief, he jumped when a hand touched his shoulder.

"Let me take over," Darren Butler said as he knelt beside him. Norman was relieved that Melissa had fetched Janet's neighbour so quickly. Mr. Butler continued treatment until June was fully breathing on her own. Norman heard sirens in the distance and rose to his knees. June opened her eyes, looked at them both, and closed them again. Her breathing seemed stable as the paramedics got out of the ambulance and ran to meet them.

Within fifteen minutes, they had stabilized her, and she was on her way to Western Memorial Hospital in Corner Brook.

As the ambulance pulled away, Norman said, "Thanks for the hand, my friend."

Darren shook his head and said, "It wasn't me, my good man. You were the one who saved her life."

* * *

A short time later, Darren stopped in front of the hospital. Norman and Melissa disembarked, the little girl holding tightly to Norman's hand as they entered the building. They waited in the lounge outside the emergency room, anxious for news on June's condition. Norman tried reaching Janet and Don on their cellphones, but both lines were busy. In the meantime, the physician on duty informed them that June would be fine.

Norman finally made contact with Janet and Don, and flight arrangements were made for them to arrive in Deer Lake that same day. Janet was at the hospital nine hours later, and Don arrived on the red-eye flight. The doctor assured them all that no damage had been done, although June had suffered a mild heart attack. When she awakened, she told them that she had felt dizzy when she was walking with Melissa by the pool and could not remember another thing until she woke up in the hospital. Janet started to cry as the story unfolded. Norman Patterson had saved her mother's life. She hugged him and whispered "Thank you" as tears flowed down her face.

* * *

Life returned to normal for Norman and the Spencer family. June recovered and was taking medication to treat her heart condition. She and Norman had become very close. Janet wished she could do something special to thank the man for what he had done. His birthday was in another month, so she spoke to Don about an idea she had.

The weeks seemed to fly by, and then June Simmons was busy making arrangements for Norman's birthday, only a few days away. She was especially thankful that she would be here to celebrate it with her family after her near-death experience.

Norman Patterson's birthday, December 15, arrived

like any other day for him, and he quickly went about his usual chores at the farm. He was beginning to enjoy life again and looked forward to each new day. Janet and her family were preparing a special supper for him that night, and he wanted to give them something to say thank you for letting him stay at their home and to become so much a part of it. He had bought them a grandfather wall clock to show his appreciation.

At four-thirty, Norman put his tools aside and went to clean up. After showering and shaving, he put on dress pants and a new shirt and made his way to the main house and knocked on the front door.

"Come in, Norman," Janet called from the kitchen. "You don't have to knock on the door. Just come on in. Please help yourself to a cocktail. Dinner will be served soon."

Norman poured himself a drink and went into the living room as Don came downstairs. Soon, the two men were deep in conversation about the new hockey season, and who would win the Stanley Cup this year. Melissa came into the room and walked over to them both and gave each one a hug. Soon, laughter filled the air as they all sat at the dining room table enjoying their meal. When the party began to settle around the table, Norman rose to offer a toast to the Spencer family, and presented them with the clock. Janet thanked him for his kindness. Her mother, June, rose and gave him an affectionate hug and thanked him again for saving her life.

As they sat back to enjoy their after-dinner coffee, Janet got up and looked at Norman. He could tell that she was going to say something important to him when he saw tears starting to form in her eyes. She gave a small cough. When she spoke, her words were full of sincerity and admiration for the man sitting next to her.

"Norm, I want you to know that we have a special place for you in our family. Not only did you save my mother's life, but you have been so good to us that we feel we have known you forever. We know also that the past few years have been very hard on you in so many ways. To show you how much we appreciate you and what you have done for us, we would like to say thank you in a special way."

Janet nodded to Norman to look over his shoulder. He seemed confused, but turned to look. His face registered shock when he saw his wife and daughter. Immediately, tears came to his eyes, and he shook his head and searched for the words that would not come. He continued to shake his head from side to side as his wife and daughter slowly walked toward him. Finally, he got up and embraced them both.

He said, "Please forgive a foolish old man for being so stupid for so many years. Please forgive me for what I have done to you."

He repeated these words as he hugged and kissed them time and time again. His wife and daughter, both crying, responded to him in kind. Around the table, all eyes were wet as they witnessed the rebirth of a family. Janet instantly knew that she and Don had made the right decision when they decided to search for their friend's family.

Norman walked to the end of the table with his long-lost family.

"How?" was all he could say as he held his wife and daughter's hands for the first time in over seven years.

Janet looked at him and said, "It was easy, Norman. You gave me back my mom's life, so I was determined to find your family and give them back to you. While I was away on business in Manitoba, I went to see some friends of mine, and they helped me locate your family."

"Thank you so much. I will never forget this, as long as I live. This Christmas is one I will never forget."

The Letter

by Lisa Ivany

It's Christmas Eve in the Baldwin home, and across the threshold, the air is festive. The archways are adorned with holly, while white, puffy garlands and red bows encircle the stairway on their ascent to the top. To the left is the living room, and occupying one spacious corner is a colossal fir tree, shimmering in its garment of shiny decorations and lights. Beneath a mantel full of green boughs and cranberry-scented candles, a fire blazes, sending flickers of warmth throughout the room.

Trevor and Nora were ecstatic when they bought this house in Robert's Arm twenty years ago. Both were twenty-four and had just graduated from university. They thought this would be a great starter home. As the years went by, however, and they raised their two girls, they felt a wonderful connection to the dwelling and decided to stay.

Trevor sits next to the fireplace, while the stereo fills the air with the soft, relaxing sound of Christmas melodies. However, he is anything but relaxed as he unfolds the letter in his hand once more. While he was looking for some gift-wrap in the bedroom closet, the letter had fallen from behind a shoebox. With a gut-wrenching sensation, he once again reads the unfamiliar script.

My Darling Nora,

I can't wait to hold you in my arms again and pick up where we left off. You're all I think about during the day and all I dream about at night. Without you, my world would be a dark place, empty of the sunshine of your love and the sweetness of your smile.

Save some mistletoe for me, sweetheart, for I will be back from my business trip on Christmas Eve, seeking the softness of your lips. I know it's difficult for you to get away, but I will wait for you.

I'll see you soon, my love.

Charles

A tear slowly cascades down Trevor's cheek as he realizes the painful implications of this letter. All these years of thinking he's the centre of Nora's universe, as she is his, have been an illusion. When did this idyllic life start to crumble? He wonders why he didn't notice the signs before, and then he realizes she has been quite evasive about her whereabouts lately. Anytime he's asked where she's been, she just says "Christmas shopping," even though she often returns home without packages. Perhaps she has been slipping out for secret trysts with this Charles fellow. He ponders who this man could be, but he can't recall anyone by that name in Nora's life.

Trevor wonders where the letter came from, as there is no accompanying envelope to reveal its point of origin. The thought crosses his mind that perhaps there are other letters. Fearing the worst, yet desperately wanting to know the truth, he climbs the stairs to their bedroom in search of more clues to this man's identity. Ransacking the closet, he's relieved to find no more love notes from Charles, though at the same time very frustrated with the lack of answers.

He hears Nora enter the front door and feels a deep sense of sadness about the upcoming confrontation. He slowly returns to the main floor and follows the sound of rattling dishes to the kitchen where Nora is preparing dinner. Unobserved, he watches her from the doorway.

She looks up with a contented smile on her face and says, "Hi, honey. I'm making berried salmon and wild rice stuffing for dinner this evening, if that's okay with you. I don't really have time to make anything more elaborate."

Sarcastically, he responds, "I guess you must want to finish early so you can meet with Charles."

"Who's Charles?"

"Nora, don't play me for a fool. I found the letter," he says as he retrieves the folded paper from his pocket and extends it toward her.

She opens the letter and immediately starts to laugh. Barely able to contain her mirth, she squeaks out, "This wasn't written to me. This is an old love letter I found in the attic a few days ago. I assume my grandfather sent it to my grandmother back when they were courting. As you know, she's the one I'm named after."

"But who is Charles? I thought your grandfather's name was Samuel."

"My grandmother married twice. Her first husband was

Charles, but he died when I was just a baby, and then my grandmother married Samuel. He's the only grandfather I've ever known."

Trevor feels his whole body go weak with this wonderful news. A short time ago he thought this would be the worst Christmas of his life, and now it feels like the best; his faith in his wife has been restored. He wraps his arms around her in a tight embrace and says, "I love you."

"I don't know if I should be mad at you for not trusting me or happy that you love me enough to be jealous." She giggles. "At least I know what to do to get your attention from now on. I'll just write myself a love letter with another man's name signed to it and leave it for you to find."

"Don't even think about it! This has been a stressful afternoon and I don't want it repeated." His brow furls as another unsettling thought enters his mind, and he must voice his concern. "Nora, lately I've been noticing that you've been gone quite often, and I was wondering where you've been going. You say you're Christmas shopping, but you come home empty-handed."

"It was supposed to be a surprise for tomorrow, but after what you've just been through, I'll show you now. Follow me," she says as she leads him down the hall toward the living room.

There, in front of the Christmas tree, is a huge package wrapped in shiny red paper and a large silver bow, addressed to Trevor. He looks at her, puzzled, and says, "Is this what you have to show me?"

"Yes. Go ahead and open it."

He walks to the package and quickly tears away the paper, to find a large portrait of his beloved wife. She's wearing a lovely red silk blouse and the diamond necklace he gave her last Christmas. Her long blonde hair is pinned on the sides, with a couple of perfectly placed curls hugging her temples.

She's beaming as she says, "You've told me many times over the years that you would like a portrait of me to go over the fireplace. For the last three months I've been going to an artist regularly to pose for this. How do you like it?"

"I think it's absolutely beautiful, but not as beautiful as the real thing." With tears in his eyes, he lays the painting to one side and gathers his wife in his arms. "Merry Christmas, my darling. I'll never doubt you again."

CHRISTMAS TRIVIA

Legends and Myths

Mistletoe

Why do we feel compelled to kiss under the mistletoe? As the legend goes, it all started with a Scandinavian goddess by the name of Frigga. Apparently, her son, Balder, was shot with an arrow made of mistletoe. Frigga was quite distraught, and while her friends were using their powers to try to save her son, she cried tears which became the white berries on the mistletoe. Balder's life was spared, and from that time on, Frigga ordered that mistletoe never be used for harm again. Instead, she started the tradition of kissing underneath it.

The Christmas Rose

When a little shepherdess came to visit the baby Jesus in His manger, she began to cry because she had no gift for Him. From each tear that fell to the ground, a lovely white rose appeared. The girl smiled and gathered the roses into a bouquet to give to the Christ Child. When Jesus touched them, the petals turned pink.

Poinsettia

Similar tales come from Mexican villages about the origin of poinsettias and their symbolism at Christmas. One version is of a young boy who plucked some dried weeds from the side of the road on his way to church service on Christmas Eve. An angel told him to place them on the altar as an offering to the baby Jesus. When the child complied, the weeds turned into the first poinsettia. It has since been called "The Flower of the Holy Night" or *Flor de la Noche Buena.*

Another version recounts the story of a little girl in a Mexican village who had no offering for the baby Jesus on Christmas Eve. She was also said to have gathered weeds by the roadside and carried them inside the church. To her embarrassment, everyone laughed at her gift as she walked up the aisle. When she placed the branches next to the manger, a miracle happened! The green leaves turned a vibrant red, and now every year the green leaves turn red.

Karrak

by Robert Hunt

It had happened again. Now the stealing was starting to get serious. Part of their food supply for winter had been taken. He noticed the animal tracks leading from the chicken coop and knew he would have to hunt the one who was raiding and killing his food stock. This was the third time this month that the animal had gotten into the coop and killed his chickens. He had spoken to many other people in the area who had also had trouble with predators robbing their winter supplies and killing their animals. To them it all seemed like the work of one animal.

Something had to be done. In this desolate area, people's very lives depended on their food supply during these long winter months, and it was the animal who raided their haunts that must die so that they would not starve.

It was Christmas Eve, and he had little time left to find and destroy his enemy. He knew the culprit that had entered, killed, and taken the chickens was a wolf. Now, the predator had to be found and destroyed.

His name was Carl Ross, but the Inuit called him Karrak,

after a great native hunter who had lived many years ago in the region. Karrak was fearless in his pursuits. When he hunted, he had always come back the victor. So, Carl knew that to live up to the name he had inherited, he would have to find and destroy the animal responsible for the killings. He would become the hunter.

Carl had come to Hopedale, Labrador, when he was a young man. His parents, John and Helen Ross, both doctors, had moved to this remote area for love of the environment, and to be close to the Atlantic Ocean. They had built a home on the peninsula, tended to the medical needs of the local people, and raised their three children. Carl's sister, Linda, and brother, Clint, had moved away several years ago, but he had become so attached to Hopedale that he decided to stay.

His father often took him hunting and fishing, and the landscape became his first love. He had known for many years that he would never leave, for this was the only life he wanted. For twenty years, he and his wife, Betty, had devoted themselves to the Inuit way of life. Their parents had done the same. This way of life had brought contentment and a happiness that they could not find in any city, so they stayed while others left.

Carl, or Karrak, followed the ways of his father and the trappers of Hopedale and learned a great deal from each of them, things that no big-city people could even begin to show him. He learned to love the land and the people, to respect the environment, and to love all God's creatures – except the one that was now stealing his winter supplies.

Karrak knew the animal was a wolf. He understood how they operated and how they hunted their prey. Sly and cunning, they were great hunters. His father had taught him that. The footprints in the snow also showed him that this wolf was a very large animal, probably weighing in excess of a hundred pounds. The hunt would be dangerous. This didn't matter to Karrak; he had hunted animals big and small since he was a young man, not for sport, but for survival.

The next day, Karrak made ready for the hunt. Early in the morning, he kissed his wife goodbye and considered the direction his instincts told him the wolf had taken. The main hunting grounds for the animal were along a place called Rigor Ridge, set low at the base of the Crystal Mountains. With any luck, he would have his kill and be back within a few hours. He had to look for a wolf with blood on its body, from its ill-gotten meat. He laced his snowshoes and started the three-mile walk to the ridge.

Along the way, he noticed several tracks, which two animals, not one, had made in the snow. It seemed that one animal was tracking the other, because one set of prints seemed to be trailing behind. Karrak stopped and studied the tracks. He knew that he had to be sure what he was up against. A cornered or rabid wolf could be very dangerous. After several moments of studying the tracks, he concluded that the wolf was dragging something with it, and was being followed by another animal. He walked ahead, and then he saw it: fresh blood, probably from the dead chickens. This would be an easy kill.

Karrak took precautions as he moved onward. He didn't know what kind of animal was trailing the wolf, so he kept his eyes trained on the second animal's prints. The trail turned and led down a small slope, and he heard a short whine. He stopped and listened, but it didn't continue. Waiting another few moments to make sure that nothing was amiss, he continued down the path until he found two fresh sets of tracks in the snow and resumed the hunt.

At one point he noticed that the wily wolf had crossed a small river to conceal its tracks, as if it sensed that another animal was following it. Karrak knew that whatever animal he was about to confront in his pursuit was a clever one. He followed the two sets of tracks for another few minutes and then noticed that they branched away from each other. As if the follower was widening its pursuit, intending to come around in front of its prey.

A light snow began to fall as Karrak pushed himself back against a tree at the end of the trail and knelt under its branches. From there, he would have a better view of another trail below, where he thought the two animals would emerge. He leaned back against the tree and waited.

What a way to spend Christmas Eve, he thought. *I should be home sitting in front of a fire.*

The hunter waited another ten minutes and then decided that the animals were not about to show themselves. He listened once more, and when he thought the way was clear, he started to move out of his hiding place. Something made him stop. Call it instinct. He stayed under the tree for another few seconds, until a wolf emerged from behind a tree not more than fifty feet ahead of him. He raised his rifle and took aim. The wolf was in his sights. Karrak didn't move, but crouched down low as he waited for the animal to move closer. In another minute or two, he would have a clear shot.

As the wolf drew closer, he saw that its side had been bloodied. It didn't matter to Karrak that it was wounded; he had to kill it to protect the community's food supplies. *It's either him or us,* he thought. He was just about to fire off a shot when something else caught his eye. He rose partway, and then saw what was to the side of the wolf. Two small cubs and another wolf, possibly the mother, were moving awkwardly away from the wounded wolf, as if they were afraid of it.

Karrak dropped his gun and moved to one side. Then he heard a cry and saw what was happening. A lynx stood only a dozen yards away from the wolf, ready to attack the wounded animal and its family. An easy kill by a more formidable foe. Karrak then surmised what the smart lynx had done. It had fought the wolf earlier and injured it, hence the blood. Somehow the wolf had gotten away, but the lynx had picked up the trail again and stayed behind the wolf long enough for it to reach its family – an added bonus.

The wolf sensed what was about to happen and readied itself to defend its family.

Just as the lynx was about to attack, Karrak raised his rifle and took aim. He fired off a shot directly above the lynx's head, and the startled animal looked once at him and then at the wolf. Then it started racing toward the wolf and its family, flinging itself into the air at the last moment for the killing strike. Karrak knew that he had only one chance. He raised the rifle again and fired. The impact flipped the lynx over backward, and it fell dead a few feet from where the wounded wolf stood in its fighting stance.

Karrak knew that he should kill all of them, but he'd had a change of heart. The only reason the wolf had raided his chickens was to provide for its family. The animal looked at Karrak and moved to protect the others. Karrak saw two chickens by the animal's side. To shoot the wolf would be to leave its family without their father and their provider.

Karrak looked at the wolf and smiled. He knew the animal's wound would heal, so he made a Christmas pact with the beast.

"Tell you what, my friend. If I let you and your family go, promise me that you'll not come back to these parts ever again. You do that for me, and you and your family can walk away from here."

The wolf looked down at the two chickens as if it understood.

"Yes, you can take the chickens with you," Karrak said.

The wolf picked up the chickens, turned, nodded its head as if in thanks, and walked away in the opposite direction.

Karrak stood there watching the wolves move toward the mountains. Then he went back to where the lynx lay, picked it up, and put it over his shoulder. He turned and walked back home to enjoy Christmas with his family.

Death Canyon Cover-up

by Lisa Ivany

"Paul, wake up!" I screamed for the third time. "I have to go home."

"What's the rush, Cassie? It's Friday night, after all," he said, his speech slurred. Seconds later, he was out cold again.

Paul lay on Colin's sofa, his black tee-shirt twisted up under his right arm, a half-empty bottle of beer dangling from his left hand. The raven-black hair which he had meticulously gelled and styled earlier was matted, and his drunken eyelids remained closed.

"Why don't you stay the night, Cassie?" a voice behind me asked. "My parents are away for the weekend."

Colin Steele leered at me from the hallway with an ominous grin. I felt exposed and vulnerable under his stare, like a deer trapped in the headlights.

"No thanks, Colin, I-I-I have to get home before curfew," I stammered.

"Well, Miss Phillips, I'm sure your parents won't mind you being a little late just this once," he said.

Without responding, I scooted out the door as though the devil were on my heels. That was probably an accurate assessment of my situation, for sure.

We were supposed to go to Colin's party for an hour and then be on our way to my aunt's annual Boxing Day dinner. Paul even promised he wouldn't drink, but, as usual, he lied. His drinking had been getting out of control, and it was sparking many arguments between us. At eighteen years of age, he wasn't old enough to drink, but he had easy access to the fully-stocked bar at home and took full advantage of it.

His parents were rarely at home, working during the day and glued to the slot machines at the local pub every night. Paul was basically raising himself, and the abundance of alcohol in the Jenkins home was too hard for the lonely teenager to resist.

I shivered in the cold winter air, in a thin jacket without a hood. I shuddered as an icy cold shiver ran up my spine. I wasn't sure whether it was from the temperature or visions of slimy Colin.

In my haste to leave his impending clutches, I'd left my scarf and gloves behind. I realized the perilous situation I was in, strutting down a dimly lit street in Portland Creek, close to midnight, completely alone. However, there was no way I was going back to that creep's house.

The next day, Paul found me on one of the Northern Peninsula's hiking trails, where the locals liked to walk or hang out. The view of the mountains was spectacular from this height. Although it was a beautiful sunny day, we were alone.

"About last night," Paul began, as he walked beside me. "Was your aunt upset that we didn't make it to dinner?"

"No. I told her we both had the flu," I answered. "I hated lying to her."

"I'm sorry to put you in that position, Cass," he said. "It won't happen again. Please give me a second chance."

"I hope you mean it this time, Paul," I snapped. "I won't cover for you again."

"You won't have to," he promised. The hike came to an abrupt halt as he pulled me into his arms and his lips found mine. The lingering softness of his mouth erased all traces of my anger.

That night, as rock music blared from the car radio, Paul drove us down the highway to a dance in Rocky Harbour. We were escorted by large pellets of hail, hammering the car. Sensing my distress with the weather situation, Paul wrapped his right arm around my shoulders while he drove with his left hand.

"You don't have to be afraid," he said soothingly. "We're riding on winter tires and the road is fairly clear anyway."

"I'd rather be in the dance hall," I murmured nervously.

"We'll be there in a few minutes," he said before pecking my lips with his.

I picked up the unmistakable odour of alcohol on his breath. Annoyed, I scooted to the other side of the seat. How could I not have known he had been drinking? He'd been slurring a lot of his words since we'd left home, and I hadn't even realized it until now. Once again, I felt like such a fool.

"How much have you had to drink tonight?" I demanded.

"Only a couple of beers," he replied.

"Tell me the truth, Paul."

"Okay, I had a few, but I'm not drunk."

"Pull over and let me take the wheel!" I shrieked. My fingers gripped tightly around the door handle.

"You're being ridiculous!" he exclaimed angrily.

"No I'm not," I yelled. "You've had too much to drink and

I will not let you drive me any farther. Stop the car or I'll jump out!"

He leaned across and grabbed my hand away from the door.

Screech! Smash!

The car had spun out of control and slammed through a guardrail. The resonating drone of the horn attracted my attention; Paul's head lay upon the steering wheel. Crimson rivulets oozed from an open wound on his forehead.

"Paul!" I wailed.

"I'm okay," he said, lifting his head. "Are you all right?"

"Yes, just a little shaken up."

The car moved, and we realized that the passenger side was teetering over a steep embankment. Being familiar with the area, known as Death Canyon, we knew we were hovering above a two-hundred-foot drop with huge boulders at the bottom. If the car were to slide over the side, it would mean death for both of us. I held my breath as though somehow it would stop the car from swaying. I knew my side of the car had nothing beneath it.

As Paul carefully extricated himself from the vehicle and extended his hand to me, the car made a terrifying lurch. He quickly dove into the car and hoisted me out of the driver's side, his arms looped around my chest. Just as my feet cleared the car, it toppled down the cliff and exploded instantly on impact. The flames from the burning wreckage provided light and I could see the tears in Paul's eyes.

"I'm so sorry, Cassie. My drinking almost cost you your life," he sniffled. "I love you, Cass, and I promise to stop drinking if you'll give me another chance."

Before I could answer, the piercing shrill of a siren and flashing red lights announced the arrival of a police car.

"What happened here?" the constable asked. His face, a pale oval in the dim light, expressed concern.

It would be *so* easy to cover for Paul again! In my mind I swiftly reviewed what might happen if I didn't. He'd lose his license. He might get fired from his job at the mill. His folks might even kick him out of the house.

"Were you driving, son?" the officer asked Paul.

"No, sir," he replied while pleading with me with his eyes to back him up.

"Is that true, miss?" the constable asked kindly. His question invited the easy answer: *Yes, officer, that's true.*

"No, it isn't," I said. My words startled me. They came out firm and clear and hung in the night air above the three of us. They surprised Paul even more.

"But Cassie . . ." he began plaintively. "You know what'll happen if –"

"I wasn't driving," I interrupted. "Paul was."

There would be no Death Canyon cover-up. I was through with lying for Paul, and even if it ended our relationship, I knew I had done the right thing and, in time, so would he.

The Ghost of Christmas

by Robert Hunt

East off Highway 70, between Carbonear and Victoria, a panorama of colour decorated most of the cemetery.

That winter, there was one particular gravesite that was not cared for. Both headstones in the plot were starting to fade with the constantly changing weather that bore down upon them and broke against the battered granite stones. The cracked paint had eroded and was peeling on the concrete. Weeds were plentiful, springing and twisting up from the ground, and beginning to interlock through the crushed stone.

Brad Long stared down at the two headstones. He hadn't noticed them before, although they were only two plots away from his brother's resting place. He was a frequent visitor to the place since his brother had passed on three years before. Strange how he had never noticed the dual plot until now.

The silence was broken by a young girl next to him. He had not seen her until a sudden movement caught his attention. She seemed lost in her thoughts as she slowly bent down and laid a small bouquet of flowers on the grave. She looked over at Brad and spoke. "My parents were both killed in a car crash several years ago. I live away from here and can't come over as much as I'd like, so the graves don't get the care they require. Do you know if there is anyone I can get to care for them?"

The first thing Brad noticed was the striking beauty of the young lady. He started to speak to her, when suddenly a swirling wind came across the graveyard and blew snow crystals into his face. He covered his eyes with his hands until it abated. When it did, a few seconds later, the young lady was gone. Brad wondered where she could have gone so quickly. She must have gone looking for the caretaker of the graveyard.

Brad finished paying his respects to his brother and started to head out of the cemetery. He hoped he would run into the young lady as he was leaving, but she was nowhere to be seen. At the entrance, he saw the caretaker and inquired about her. The gentleman in charge said that no one had approached him about caring for any grave. Brad was just about to get into his car when the girl appeared on the other side of the passenger door and spoke to him.

"Hi, my name is Gail Hudson. I'm sorry to bother you again, but I noticed that you care for your brother's grave, and you have done a magnificent job of it. Would I be able to interest you in taking care of my parents' plot as well? I'll pay you well for the work you do. I spoke to the caretaker, and he said that it's left to family members to take care of their plots. Because I live away, I won't be able to do so. Would it be too much to ask you to care for it?"

Brad looked at the young woman and knew that he

couldn't say no. His heart wouldn't allow him to do it. He would be doing two gravesites the next time he came here.

He said, "I'll look after your parents' plot free of charge. There's not a lot of work to be done with it anyway. In the summer, I'll cut the grass and add a little paint here and there. It'll be my pleasure to do this for you, and for your parents."

She looked at him with admiration in her eyes. "Thank you, sir. That's so kind of you, but I insist on paying for the paint. Here's my address and home phone number," she said as she scribbled on a piece of paper. "Please feel free to contact me concerning anything you need for the plot," she continued, "and I'll make sure that it's provided for you. You can also contact my uncle who lives here in the city. His number and address are below mine. Again, thanks very much."

Brad told her she was welcome and got in his car and drove away. The young woman was so beautiful! He would love to see her again. Maybe, if he needed some money for renovations for the grave, their paths would cross again. He thought it strange that she said she had spoken to the care-taker of the graveyard when the gentleman said that no one had. Brad shrugged. The caretaker must have forgotten about the conversation. He left the cemetery with thoughts of the young lady in his mind.

* * *

Four months later, Brad had turned the Hudsons' plot into a wonderful sight to behold. He had trimmed the grass, painted the concrete, and touched up the headstones. He added flowers to decorate the top of the graves. All the while, his thoughts were on Gail Hudson; he wondered if he would ever see her again. She was just a phone call away, but he thought that might be rude; he had already told her that he wouldn't need anything for the grave's upkeep. Well, maybe next year she would visit again.

The months passed quickly, and though Brad tried, he could not get the beautiful vision of Gail Hudson out of his head. He had given in and called the number she gave him but had no luck contacting her, as the number had been disconnected. She must have made a mistake when she gave it to him. He could phone the uncle, but he decided against it. It had taken all his courage just to dial her number.

It was getting very close to Christmas. About three centimetres of snow had fallen, and everything had taken on a Christmas air. Brad loved this time of year, the celebration and merriment that were a part of the holidays. Christmas Day was just around the corner, and he had many things to do before he could start his holidays.

Brad was so deep in thought that he didn't realize he was driving toward the cemetery. He stopped his car when he got there and decided to pay his respects at his brother's grave. Stepping out of the car, he headed down the small road that led a few hundred yards or so to the plot. He quickened his pace and soon made the turn and was standing in front of his brother's snow-covered grave. Saying a quick prayer, he turned to head back to his car, when he almost dropped to his knees in fright as he noticed the Hudsons' dual plot.

Brad rubbed his eyes. It couldn't be! There had to be some mistake. The plot was just as he had left it four months before. Not only was it the same, but it was the only gravesite not covered in snow. Brad walked over to it, his mind racing as he tried to make sense of what he was seeing. The grass was still growing on the plot, even though it was winter! It was impossible! It had to be some kind of hallucination.

Brad shut his eyes and turned his back to the plot. He hoped that when he opened them again there would be snow on top of the graves; he had to be imagining this. Turning slowly, he opened his eyes. He wasn't going insane after all. The plot was as snow-covered as the rest of the graves. He was so relieved, he sat down on the edge of his brother's grave.

As Brad got ready to leave the graveyard, he made a mental note to talk to Gail's uncle and see if he could somehow put him in touch with her. After all, Brad did need more paint for the upcoming summer to care for the Hudson plot, and Gail had said that he could contact her if he needed supplies.

He walked around the corner of the Hudsons' graves, when something caught his eye. He had to crouch at the edge of the grave to read the headstone. Brad stared at the headstone, shivering as he read..

GAIL HUDSON, AGE 20, DIED TRAGICALLY
ON NOVEMBER 23, 2002. MAY HER SOUL REST IN PEACE.

Without looking, Brad remembered that the Hudsons had died on the same day, in an automobile accident! It dawned on him that he had been talking to a ghost or apparition many months before!

Brad rushed from the graveyard, knowing what he had to do. He went to the library and looked up the death notices in the microfiche for the date of November 23, 2002. His hands shook as he went through the pages of the newspaper and stopped on the date he was looking for. There, beneath bold headlines on the second page, was a picture of the Hudsons. It read:

PROMINENT BUSINESSMAN AND FAMILY
TRAGICALLY KILLED ON THE TRANS-CANADA HIGHWAY
NEAR THE TURNOFF TO CARBONEAR.

Brad started to read the story, and when he looked at the second picture provided, he sat back in shock. It showed Gail Hudson and her parents, the same Gail Hudson he had met in the graveyard last year.

Brad knew then that Gail Hudson had come to ask him to tend to her parents' graves before she could finally rest in peace.

CHRISTMAS TRIVIA

Christmas Traditions of the World

Spanish Christmas

In Spain, Christmas is a religious holiday, and begins on December 8 for the feast of the Immaculate Conception. Each year there is a celebration in front of the gothic cathedral in Seville, where the "dance of six" is performed by ten boys in costume.

Christmas Eve is known as the "Good Night," and at this time family members gather for a feast around a nativity, which is common in most homes.

One Spanish belief is that the Magi still travel to Bethlehem each year at Christmas. Children put their shoes on windowsills and fill them with carrots, straw, and barley for the Wise Men's horses.

December 28 is the feast of the Holy Innocents, when young boys light bonfires and one of them plays the role of mayor of the town. He orders the people to perform duties, and if they refuse, they are fined.

Portuguese Christmas

In Portugal, Christmas is observed very similar to the way it is in Spain. They have, however, an extra feast called Consoada. Early on Christmas Day they set extra places at the table for "the souls of the dead." Some homes leave crumbs on the hearth for these souls in the hope of a good harvest.

Chinese Christmas

Homes in China are lit with paper lanterns and decorated Christmas trees which they call Trees of Light. They are draped with paper chains, paper lanterns, and paper flowers. Children hang stockings and wait for Santa Claus to visit, whom they call "Christmas Old Man."

The Chinese New Year begins near the end of January and is now called the Spring Festival. At this time, children receive new clothing and toys, and have luxurious meals. They also enjoy displays of fireworks. Portraits of ancestors are hung in the main room of the home.

Unexpected Gift

by Lisa Ivany

"Forget it, Martha, I'm not going on a blind date with your nephew!" exclaimed Julie Marshall, brushing snow off her car. Long tendrils of wavy chestnut hair had escaped from beneath her cap, to surround an attractive and somewhat delicate face with eyes the shade of sapphires. Her heavy black ski jacket failed to conceal the slender figure and petite frame beneath. "I know you mean well, but my track record with men is abysmal, and I'm not ready to set myself up for disappointment again."

"But Julie, D.J. is a wonderful guy with a great personality. He's also sensitive, humorous, and a hopeless romantic. What more could you want?"

"If he's so well-endowed, why is he still single at thirty-five?" Julie queried skeptically.

"Maybe he's just waiting for the right girl to come along. Besides, you're still single at thirty-five and there's nothing wrong with you," Martha said, chuckling. "If you change your mind, he's listed in the telephone directory under D.J. Sterling, or I can get him to call you."

Shrugging her shoulders, Julie felt she was losing a battle of wills. Reluctantly, she said, "I'll think about it and let you know in the new year. It's Christmas Eve and I really have to finish my last-minute shopping. I'll see you later."

With a satisfied smile, Martha called out as she headed to her house next door, "Don't forget, dinner's at six tomorrow."

As Julie drove by the snow-covered houses with their decorations and coloured lights, she felt a sense of loneliness. This had been her favourite holiday, before the terrible car accident which claimed the lives of the rest of her family nearly ten years ago. Her parents and younger sister died at the scene, and her older brother was sustained on life support for two days, before finally slipping away. They were all going out for a family dinner, but Julie was called in to work at the last minute and couldn't join them. She often wished she had been in the car that day, rather than living every day since with the heartache of such loss.

After that tragic time, she left her hometown of Harbour Breton, and headed to Alberta to try to distance herself from the painful reminders of her beloved family. She found employment as a receptionist in one of the local accounting firms and submerged herself in work, but try as she might, this did little to fill the void in her life.

She was blessed to have Fred and Martha Ryan living next door, and even though they tended to meddle in her life, their hearts were in the right place. If not for their kindness, she would undoubtedly have spent many Christmases alone.

Pulling into the mall parking lot, she had to circle around several times before she was finally able to find a place to park. Apparently, she was not the only last-minute shopper in town.

Inside the mall, she marvelled at the spectacular Christmas displays in each shop. Poinsettias, holly, and mistletoe graced the windows, while inside there were Christmas trees adorned with different variations of ornaments and twinkling lights. The festive atmosphere pulled at the corners of Julie's lips, although her smile didn't seem to reach her eyes.

Entering Diamond Jewellers, she browsed through the cabinets and showcases until she spied an exquisite pair of gold hoop earrings embedded with tiny diamonds. They would make a lovely gift for Martha, and she decided to buy a pair for herself as well. She already pictured how striking they would look with her new black suit. Her thoughts were interrupted when a salesman appeared.

"May I be of assistance?" he asked.

"Yes, I would like to buy two pairs of these earrings, please."

"I'm sorry, madam, but this is the only pair we have left in this style."

"Oh well, I'll buy this pair for my friend then."

After spending most of the day standing in lengthy lineups, hunger pangs reminded her she had forgotten to have lunch. The drive home would take an hour, and she didn't want to wait that long to eat. With her arms full of cumbersome packages, she looked for somewhere to eat, and entered Dan's Steak House. She had never dined there before, but had heard good things about the place.

Barely able to see over the bundle in her arms, she stumbled into a nearby table, capsizing an adjacent chair. In an effort to keep her balance, she dropped her shopping bags and watched helplessly as their contents scattered over the floor.

Stooping down hurriedly, she retrieved her purchases,

feeling her cheeks start to burn from her undignified entry into the busy restaurant. Suddenly, she was aware of an extra pair of hands gathering her packages and passing them along to her. She thanked the gentleman for his help and scurried toward the front door, barely acknowledging his presence in her current state of embarrassment.

He called out to her, "Excuse me, but you've missed one of your packages."

Julie reluctantly returned for the item and noticed him for the first time. Not a handsome face, but rather one that was ruggedly attractive, crested with a thick swatch of black, silky hair, and certainly worthy of a woman's curiosity. There was an amiable glint in his brown eyes, and a magnetic smile crossed an unblemished expanse of pearl-white teeth as he held out Julie's shopping bag.

A tingling heat suffused her body that had nothing to do with the temperature or her recent debacle. Coming back to the moment, she accepted the object with gratitude while trying to maintain a hold on her awkward bundle.

"Thank you so much for your help. It's nice to see chivalry is still alive," Julie commented.

"You're kindly welcome," he replied. "May I ask why you're leaving?"

"I'm just noticing how full this place is, and I assume it will take quite a while to get served. Besides, I thought I'd make a quick retreat after the spectacle I just made of myself."

"I'm sure no one even noticed," he said with an enticing grin. "Regarding your order, I can guarantee you won't have long to wait, and I would be honoured if you would join me for lunch. I happen to be sitting at the best table in the house."

"With an offer like that, how can I refuse?" she smiled.

"By the way, my name is Danny," he said. He relieved her of her packages and led her to a festively adorned table in a secluded corner.

"I'm Julie."

"Well, Julie, would you like a menu?" he asked.

"Actually, I already know what I want," she replied. "The famous Dan Burger platter I've heard so much about from the girls at the office."

"Good choice," he said. "Would you excuse me for a moment?"

"Sure," she responded as she removed her jacket and set about squeezing some of her smaller packages into the larger bags. Within a few minutes, Danny was back, bearing two platters. Julie's look was one of astonishment as she asked, "How did we get our food so quickly, and why didn't the waitress bring it?"

With a sheepish grin, Danny said, "It helps when you're the owner."

"You own this place?"

"Owner, waiter, bottle washer, you name it," he chuckled. "Where do you think the name Dan Burger comes from?"

Julie grinned. "It must be so nice to have a hamburger named after you." Taking a bite, she exclaimed, "This is fabulous! Is it a secret recipe?"

"Not really, but if I tell you, I'll have to kill you," Danny bantered.

Two hours later, after a delightfully relaxed and pleasant afternoon, Julie reluctantly prepared to leave. She opened her wallet, but Danny insisted the meal was on the house and she gratefully accepted. She thanked him for his generosity, and as she gathered her belongings, he grinned mischievously, saying, "Try not to trip over anything on the way out."

While driving home, Julie played over the afternoon in her mind. She couldn't remember the last time she had enjoyed herself so thoroughly or laughed so much. To her, Christmas had always been a sad time filled with loneliness, in contrast to the joy it created for most. She switched on the radio and the car's interior filled with the tune "I'll Be Home For Christmas." Her recent exhilaration changed to melancholy as the words of this famous carol reminded her of the family she would never share Christmas with again.

That evening, while wrapping presents, Julie could not find the earrings she bought for Martha. She searched all the shopping bags, her handbag, and the car, and retracing her steps, all to no avail. They must have fallen out in the restaurant, but now it was too late to check as it was closed for the holidays. Julie went to her jewellery box. Inside, she uncovered a faux pearl necklace given to her last Christmas which she had never worn. Feeling this to be the perfect gift, she placed it in a velvet box and returned to her task of gift-wrapping.

Later that night, she had difficulty falling asleep; not from the excitement of Christmas Eve, but due to the constant images of Danny's face moving beneath her lids. She realized she didn't even know his last name, nor did he know hers. Any hope of receiving a call from him was quickly extinguished by this thought, and she dared not return to the restaurant for fear he would think she was pursuing him. She did have her pride, after all! Perhaps he was married anyway. Sadly, she drifted off to sleep, resigning herself to another lonely Christmas.

The following evening, as Julie entered the foyer of the house next door, Martha conspiratorially pulled her to one side and whispered, "Julie, I want to tell you before you come in that my nephew is also here for dinner. Believe me, this is not a set-up. He was supposed to be at his sister's, but her kids have all come down with chicken pox, and since he has never had it, he felt it best not to go there. He called to see if it was okay to come here, and of course I was delighted. I hope you don't mind."

"That's okay, Martha. It's not like it's a date, and it *is* Christmas, after all."

"Well, I have to go to the kitchen and make sure Fred's not stuffing himself on turkey. Why don't you go into the living room and introduce yourself to D.J.?"

Julie walked down the hallway, and as she rounded the corner, her gaze was drawn to the man sitting by the fireplace. She couldn't believe her eyes! In front of her was the man who had tortured her dreams the previous night.

She exclaimed, "Danny, you're Martha's nephew, D.J.?"

"Yes," he replied in equal astonishment. "I had no idea you were the neighbour she wanted me to meet! If I had known, I would have been knocking on your door a long time ago."

She grinned. "And I certainly would have answered."

"Incidentally, I have something in my jacket to show you," he said. "I'll be right back."

When he returned, he extended a small package to her.

"After you left the restaurant yesterday, I found these earrings on the table and wondered if they were yours."

"Yes, they are. I bought them as a Christmas gift for Martha, but I have something else for her now."

"Well, I think they would look stunning on you with that lovely outfit you're wearing."

Simultaneously, they both noticed the mistletoe they were standing beneath. Without a word, he slowly bent forward and captured her lips in a soft kiss.

"Merry Christmas, Julie. May all your holiday wishes come true," he murmured.

"I think they already have," she whispered in return. Indeed, she felt some of the sadness lift from her heart and a wonderful feeling of warmth envelop her as she looked into his eyes. She thought maybe this Christmas she would find the unexpected gift of love which had eluded her for so long, and perhaps her heart would finally start to heal.

CHRISTMAS TRIVIA

Legends and Myths

Robin's Red Breast

On the night Jesus was born, a little brown bird was watching from the rafters of the stable. A cold breeze blew in during the night and Joseph built a fire to keep the baby warm.

As the bird watched from above, she noticed the fire was going out so she flew down to fan it out. She flapped her wings until morning, and the heat of the fire turned her feathered chest a bright shade of red.

The breast of the robin has remained red since that night, as a sign of a little bird's love for the newborn king.

Nutcracker

Two boys were gathering hazelnuts in a forest one day long ago. When they sat down under a tree, they realized the nuts were too hard to crack with their teeth. A funny-looking dwarf came by who had a large head, red coat, and yellow cap, and a long, black pigtail hanging down his back.

The boys asked the dwarf if he would be able to crack their nuts. He promised to do this if they would give him some of them.

They agreed and he told them to place the nuts in his mouth and pull on his long pigtail. After placing the nuts in his mouth and pulling on his hair, the nuts were cracked.

When the little nutcracker man asked the boys for his share of the nuts, they refused and he became very angry. His face turned red with rage. He pulled on his own pigtail and bit off their heads.

St. Bernard

You may be wondering what a St. Bernard has to do with Christmas lore, but there actually is a connection. According to legend, these hefty dogs carried food and drink in small barrels or leather bags around their necks in the cold winter to people they rescued in the Swiss Alps. That's probably why Santa Claus decided a St. Bernard would make a great pet and brought one home to the North Pole. Because of the little barrel of apple cider the dog wore around his neck for the elves, Santa named him Cider.

Christmas Recipes

MAIN COURSES
SIDE DISHES
APPETIZERS
DESSERTS

Tired of eating leftover turkey from Christmas to New Year's? Well, here's a selection of some of my favourite dishes that I cook during the festive season to keep my taste buds from becoming bored. Many have been the hit of holiday potlucks as well. I hope you enjoy them as much as I do.

If you have any questions or comments regarding the recipes in this book, please feel free to contact me at livany@nf.sympatico.ca.

Merry Christmas and Happy Dining!
Lisa Ivany

Recipes

FRUIT DIP

8 oz. cream cheese, softened
7 oz. jar marshmallow cream
2 tbsp. milk
1/8 tsp. lemon juice

In small bowl, cream together all ingredients. Serve with assorted fruits.

CRANBERRY DIP

14 oz. can jellied cranberry sauce
2 tsp. lemon juice
1/2 tsp. prepared mustard
2 tbsp. sugar

Whisk all ingredients together and place in small serving bowl. Great served with Bacon Wiener Bites or with meatballs, chicken fingers, or fruit.

DILL DIP

1 cup mayonnaise
1 cup sour cream
1 small onion, chopped fine
1 tin flaked ham, mashed
1 tbsp. dillweed
3 tbsp. dried parsley
Italian bread loaf
6 onion bagels

Combine mayonnaise, sour cream, onion, ham, dillweed, and parsley.

Scoop out Italian loaf and pour dip inside. Cut scooped-out bread into cubes or chunks to use for dipping. Also, cut up bagels in chunks for dipping.

Variation: Pumpernickel bread may be used instead of Italian.

TACO MEAT DIP

1 1/2 lbs. lean ground beef
4 tbsp. taco seasoning (1 packet)
bottle taco sauce
large onion, chopped
1 cup sour cream
6 green onions, chopped
3 medium tomatoes, chopped
2 1/2 cups shredded cheddar cheese

Preheat oven to 350°.

Fry meat with large onion; add taco seasoning and 3/4 cup water. Bring to a boil and simmer, uncovered, about 10 minutes, stirring occasionally. Drain.

Line ungreased 9" x 13" pan with meat mixture. Pour taco sauce over meat.

Combine sour cream, green onions, and tomatoes. Spread this mixture over taco sauce layer. Sprinkle with cheese and bake 15–20 minutes or until cheese is melted, but not browned.
Serve hot with nacho chips as dippers.

BACON WIENER BITES

12 wieners
16 thin slices of bacon
1/4 cup packed brown sugar

Preheat oven to 250°.

Cut each wiener into 4 pieces and each bacon slice into 3 pieces. Wrap each wiener with a piece of bacon, securing with a toothpick. Roll in brown sugar to coat each side. Arrange in single layer on a cookie sheet lined with greased foil wrap.

Bake 1 1/2 hours. Serve warm either with or without your favourite dipping sauce. May be cooled and frozen. To reheat, bake in 350° oven until bacon starts to sizzle.

WON TON CUPS

24 won ton wrappers, thawed
1 1/3 cups finely shredded cheddar cheese
2/3 cup chopped pecans
1/2 tsp. onion powder
1/2 cup salad dressing or mayonnaise
2 tbsp. very finely diced red pepper
1 tbsp. snipped chives

Preheat oven to 350°.

Spray miniature muffin pans with cooking spray (for 24 count).

Place a 3-inch-round cookie cutter on top of a won ton wrapper.

With the cookie cutter as the guide, cut a circle out of the wrapper with a sharp steak knife. Repeat until 24 circles have been cut. Place each circle into sprayed miniature muffin pans and press bottom and sides to form a cup.

Bake 6–8 minutes or until wrappers are light golden brown; set aside.

In a small bowl, combine cheese, pecans, onion powder, salad dressing, and red pepper. Combine well and spoon into won ton cups (about 1 heaping teaspoon per cup). Sprinkle with chopped chives. Garnish with a sliver of red pepper if desired.

Either serve cold or allow to stand at room temperature 1–2 hours for crispy cups. Cups may soften if left at room temperature too long. A great finger food for parties.

SWEET AND SOUR MEATBALLS

1 box frozen Swedish meatballs
1 1/2 cups brown sugar
4 tsp. dry mustard
1/2 cup vinegar

Cook meatballs according to package directions and drain off fat. Combine remaining ingredients and pour over meatballs. Cook in oven or microwave until heated through.

HOT BACON CHEESE DIP

1 loaf round bread
12 slices bacon, fried crisp and crumbled
1 1/4 cups shredded Tex Mex cheese
3/4 cup grated Parmesan cheese
1 1/4 cups real mayonnaise
1 small onion, finely chopped
1 tsp. garlic powder
1/4 cup sour cream

Preheat oven to 375°.

Cut slice from top of bread horizontally. Hollow out centre of loaf, leaving about a 1-inch-thick shell. Cut removed bread into bite size cubes; set aside in plastic bag.

Combine remaining ingredients in medium bowl, stirring well. Transfer to hollowed bread bowl and cover with the top slice that was cut off. Cover entire loaf with foil wrap and place on a cookie sheet.

Bake 1 hour 20 minutes, or until heated through. Serve with bread cubes and crackers.

To reheat, microwave filled bread with top on high for 1–2 minutes or until heated through.

CHEESY BACON SLICES

4 1/2 cups shredded medium cheddar cheese
6–8 slices bacon, fried and crumbled*
1/2 tsp. onion powder
2/3 cup salad dressing or mayonnaise
2 tbsp. chopped green onions or chives
2 baguettes, cut into 20 slices each

Combine first 5 ingredients in bowl; stir well to combine. Spread mixture over one side of baguette slices and broil in oven until cheese is melted.

* 1/2 package of real bacon bits can be substituted.

TORTELLINI CAESAR SALAD

From the story "Lucky's Discovery"

3 cups cold cooked cheese tortellini
1 head romaine lettuce, chopped
creamy Caesar dressing
croutons
bacon bits
grated Parmesan cheese

Combine tortellini and lettuce. Toss with dressing and top with croutons, bacon bits, and Parmesan cheese according to your personal taste.

CRANBERRY CARROTS

6 carrots, sliced into thin coins
1/4 cup butter or margarine
1/4 cup jellied cranberry sauce
salt
Cook carrots; set aside. Place butter in microwave casserole dish. Cook, covered, on high for 1 minute. Add cranberry sauce. Cook, covered, 1 minute, until sauce is melted. Stir; add carrots. Cook on high 4–5 minutes. Season with salt to taste.

ROASTED VEGETABLES

From the story "Lucky's Discovery"

2–3 large potatoes
4 carrots
1 small turnip
2 stalks celery
1 yellow or red onion
1/2 red pepper
seasoning salt
pepper
garlic powder

Preheat oven to 350°.

Cut potatoes, carrots, turnip, and celery into stew-size chunks and place on cookie sheet or baking pan. Cut onion into about 8 wedges and red pepper into chunks and add to other vegetables. Sprinkle with seasonings, to desired taste. Pour about 2–3 tbsp. olive oil over vegetables and stir to combine. Bake 1 hour.

WILD RICE STUFFING

From the story "The Letter"

6 1/2 oz. package long grain and wild rice mix
2 tbsp. butter or hard margarine
1/2 cup chopped celery
1/2 cup chopped onion
10 oz. can mushroom pieces, drained
1/4 tsp. salt
1/2 tsp. poultry seasoning

Cook rice according to package directions.

Heat butter in frying pan. Add celery and onion. Sauté until soft. Add mushrooms, salt, and poultry seasoning. Stir. Add to cooked rice and mix well. Makes about 3 1/2 cups, enough to serve 4 as a side dish or to stuff 4 Cornish hens.

CHEDDAR CHOWDER

2 cups diced turnip
1 1/2 cups diced carrot
1 cup diced onion
3/4 cup diced celery
2 cups chicken broth
1/2 tsp. salt
1/4 tsp. pepper
1 cup diced potato
2 cups shredded medium cheddar cheese

Combine first 7 ingredients into a large saucepan and bring to a boil. Cover and simmer 15 minutes and then add potato. Cover and continue to simmer 15 minutes more or until vegetables are tender. Do not drain. Add cheese and stir until melted.

CHEESE LOAF

From the story "Lucky's Discovery"

1/2 cup butter or hard margarine
4 oz. cream cheese, softened
1/4 tsp. onion powder
1/4 tsp. garlic powder
1 cup shredded 4-cheese Italiano cheese*
1 1/2 tsp. dried parsley flakes
1 loaf French bread, cut into 15 slices

Preheat oven to 350°.

With electric mixer, beat butter, cream cheese, onion powder, and garlic powder. Stir in cheese and parsley.

Spread cheese mixture on both sides of each bread slice, keeping loaf on long sheet of foil wrap (over double the length of the loaf). Reshape loaf and wrap foil completely around bread, folding ends to seal completely.

Bake 30 minutes or until cheese has melted and bread is hot. Makes 15 slices.

CARROT RING

2 lbs. carrots
1/2 cup milk
1 cup bread crumbs
1 1/2 cups shredded medium Cheddar cheese
2 tsp. dried parsley flakes
1 tsp. seasoned salt
3 large eggs, fork-beaten
1/8 tsp. pepper

Preheat oven to 350°.

Cook carrots in boiling water with a sprinkle of salt until tender. Drain. Mash finely (you should get about 3 cups when mashed).

Transfer carrots to a large bowl and add remaining ingredients, mixing well. Spray a small tube pan with cooking spray and add carrot mixture, smoothing the top. Bake 45–50 minutes, until knife inserted in centre comes out clean. Let stand in pan 10 minutes before turning out onto serving plate.

SMASHED POTATOES

2 lbs. baby Yukon Gold or red potatoes
1/2 cup sour cream
2 tbsp. butter or margarine
3 slices bacon, cooked crisp and crumbled
salt and pepper to taste

Place potatoes in medium pot and cut larger potatoes in half, leaving skins on. Cover with water and bring to a boil (for a faster boil, do this with lid on). Salt the water and continue to boil another 10–11 minutes with lid off, until tender.

Drain potatoes and return to hot pot. Smash with sour cream, butter, and bacon. Season the smashed potatoes with salt and pepper. If they are too thick, thin them out with milk or a splash of broth.

TWICE-BAKED POTATOES

From the story "A Paramedic's Nightmare"

4 baking potatoes
3 green onions, finely chopped
2 tbsp. butter or margarine
1/2 cup hot milk
1/2 tsp. salt
1/8 tsp. pepper
1/4 tsp. paprika
4 slices bacon, fried crisp
2 tbsp. grated Parmesan cheese
2 tbsp. shredded cheddar cheese

Preheat oven to 400°.

Wash potatoes and pat dry. Prick each potato in several places with a fork.

Bake for about 1 hour, or until potatoes are done. Reduce oven temperature to 375°. Cut a thin slice from the top of each potato and scoop out the pulp, leaving about 1/4" shell. Mash pulp with hot milk in medium bowl until fluffy. Beat in the butter and green onion; add seasonings.

Crumble bacon and add to potato mixture. Divide mixture evenly among the potato shells. Sprinkle with Parmesan cheese and then cheddar cheese. Place potatoes on baking sheet and return to oven until cheese is melted and potatoes are hot, about 15 minutes. Serve immediately.

BERRIED SALMON

From the story "The Letter"

4 salmon steaks or fillets
Real mayonnaise (not light)
1/4 cup partridgeberries or blueberries
2–3 tbsp. maple syrup
salt and pepper to taste

Preheat oven to 325°.

Sprinkle salt and pepper over salmon; then spread a layer of mayo over top. Sprinkle with berries and then maple syrup.

Bake, uncovered for 30 minutes (or up to 40 minutes if salmon is thick). Do not turn.

BROCCOLI FISH BAKE

10 oz. frozen broccoli spears or 1 lb. fresh, cut in spears
1 lb. cod fillet
10 oz. can cream of broccoli soup
1/3 cup milk
1 cup grated cheddar cheese

1 cup dry bread crumbs
4 tbsp. soft tub margarine, melted
1/8 tsp. paprika

Preheat oven to 450°.

Cook broccoli until still a little firm.
In 7" x 11" shallow baking dish, arrange broccoli. Top with fish. In small bowl, mix soup and milk and pour over fish.

Sprinkle cheese over soup mixture. Mix bread crumbs, margarine, and paprika and sprinkle over cheese.

Bake 20 minutes or until fish flakes easily when tested with a fork. Serve over rice.

BREADED COD

4 - 4 oz. cod fillets
1/2 cup sour cream
1 tbsp. onion soup mix (stir before measuring)
1/2 cup bread crumbs
1 tbsp. grated Parmesan cheese
1/8 tsp. paprika
sprinkle dillweed or seafood seasoning
2 tbsp butter or margarine, melted
4 lemon wedges, optional

Preheat oven to 500°.

In shallow bowl, combine sour cream and soup mix. In separate shallow bowl, combine bread crumbs, Parmesan cheese, paprika, and dillweed. Dip fish in sour cream mixture and then bread crumb mixture to coat completely. Arrange in a greased dish in single layer. Drizzle with melted butter.

Bake 10–12 minutes or until fish flakes easily when tested with a fork. Squeeze juice from lemon wedge if desired.

EASY BAKED BEANS

3 - 14 oz. bottles Clark baked beans*
3 slices bacon, chopped in 1/2-inch pieces
1 medium red onion, finely chopped
3 tbsp. store-bought barbecue sauce
1 tbsp. brown sugar, optional

Preheat oven to 425°.

Pour beans into a 2L casserole dish and add barbecue sauce; stir to combine well. Place casserole in oven.

In a small, non-stick skillet, cook bacon over medium-high heat, about 2–3 minutes. Add onions and cook 5–6 minutes longer. Take beans out of the oven and scatter onions, bacon, and brown sugar over top of beans. Return to oven and bake 10 minutes. Stir beans to combine topping throughout.

* Canned baked beans can be substituted for the bottled beans.

ASIAN WINGS

2 tbsp. olive oil
12 whole chicken wings
salt and pepper
3/4 cup plum sauce
1/2 cup orange juice
1/4 tsp. ginger powder
1 1/2 tbsp. soya sauce
1/4 tsp. crushed chilies

Preheat oven to 400°.

Heat oil in large skillet over high heat. Season wings with salt and pepper to taste. Once pan is very hot, add wings in single layer (do in two batches if necessary). Brown wings about 4–5 minutes per side.

In a small saucepan over high heat, combine plum sauce, orange juice, ginger, soya sauce, and crushed chilies. Bring to a boil and then simmer while wings are cooking.

When wings are browned, transfer to oven-safe pan and pour sauce over top. Bake, uncovered, 30 minutes, turning halfway through cooking.

SWEET AND SOUR THIGHS

1 cup grape jelly
3/4 cup ketchup
1/2 onion, chopped fine
2 tbsp. white vinegar

1 tsp. dry mustard
3 lbs. chicken thighs, skin removed

Preheat oven to 350°.

In a small saucepan, stir together grape jelly, ketchup, onions, vinegar, and dry mustard. Heat over medium-high heat until mixture comes to a boil and jelly is melted. Remove from heat.

Arrange chicken pieces in 9" x 13" baking dish. Sprinkle with salt. Pour sauce evenly over chicken and turn pieces to coat both sides. Bake, uncovered, for 1–1 1/2 hours, until chicken is very tender.

CHIP TENDERS

1 lb. chicken tenders,
or boneless breast cut in 3" strips
1 cup flour
seasoned salt
pepper
1 egg
2 tbsp. milk
200g bag ridged potato chips,
sour cream and onion flavor, finely crushed

Preheat oven to 350°.

Sprinkle chicken tenders with seasoned salt and pepper. Using three shallow dishes, place flour in one, egg fork-beaten with milk in another, and crushed chips in the last one. Coat tenders in flour mixture, then in egg, and finally in crushed chips.

Place coated chicken onto sprayed wire rack of broiler pan or place on a wire rack over a cookie sheet. (Make sure the rack is sprayed with cooking spray to prevent chicken from sticking.)

Bake 22–25 minutes, or until cooked through and lightly browned. Great served with plum sauce or any dipping sauce you prefer.

These should make about 12 tenders. They can also be cut smaller to use as appetizers.

CHICKEN WITH MUSHROOM SAUCE

4 bone-in chicken breasts, skin removed
sprinkle salt
sprinkle paprika
sprinkle salt-free spice of your choice
1/4 cup chicken broth

Mushroom Sauce:

3 tbsp. butter or margarine
1 cup chopped onion
2 cups chopped fresh mushrooms
2 tbsp. flour
1/2 tsp. salt
1/8 tsp. pepper
1 tsp. paprika
1 tsp. sugar
1 1/4 cups milk
Preheat oven to 325°.

Spray casserole dish well with cooking spray. Season breasts with salt, paprika, and salt-free spice. Place in single layer in casserole and add chicken broth. Bake, uncovered, 30 minutes. Cover and continue baking 40 minutes.

Meanwhile, for mushroom sauce, melt butter in small heavy saucepan. Add onion. Sauté 4–5 minutes and add mushroom pieces. Sauté until onions are soft and clear. Combine flour, salt, pepper, paprika, and sugar. Stir into onion/mushroom mixture. Stir in milk until it boils and thickens. Spoon over chicken.

BROCCOLI AND CHICKEN CASSEROLE

From the story "A Paramedic's Nightmare"

2–3 chicken breasts
10 oz. frozen broccoli spears
10 oz. can cream of mushroom soup
1/3 cup mayonnaise
1/2 cup grated cheddar cheese
1/2 tsp. lemon juice
1 cup bread crumbs
3 tbsp. melted butter

Preheat oven to 350°.

Cook chicken until it comes off the bones and then cube. Cook broccoli 10 minutes.

Line greased 3L casserole with broccoli and cover with chicken cubes.

Combine soup, mayonnaise, and lemon juice and pour over chicken. Sprinkle with cheese. Combine bread crumbs and butter and spread over cheese. Bake 30 minutes.

ONE POT PORK CHOPS

4 pork chops
6 small carrots, cut julienne style
2 stalks celery, cut julienne style
1 onion, chopped
6–8 small potatoes, quartered
salt to taste
2 - 10 oz. cans tomato soup
1 cup water
2 tsp. Worcestershire sauce

In skillet, brown chops; drain fat. Add vegetables and sprinkle with salt. In medium bowl, combine soup, water, and Worcestershire sauce. Pour over vegetables. Cover and cook over low heat 45 minutes or until tender.

DAN BURGER

From the story *"Unexpected Gift"*

1 lb. lean ground beef
1/4 cup Corn Flake crumbs
1/4 cup bread crumbs
1 egg
1 tbsp. salad dressing or mayo
1 tsp. Worcestershire sauce

1 tsp. brown sugar
1/2 tsp. seasoned salt
1/2 tsp. Montreal steak spice
1/4 cup barbecue sauce
1/4 cup Thousand Island dressing
1 small red onion, sliced
6 slices bacon, cut in half
4 slices Monterey Jack cheese
4 tomato slices
shredded lettuce
4 sesame seed hamburger buns, buttered

Combine first 9 ingredients until blended and form into four wide flat patties. Grill on barbecue or indoor grill 5 minutes per side.

Sauté red onion and fry bacon until crisp.

Just before burgers are ready to remove from the grill, place 1 tbsp. of barbecue sauce on each one and then a cheese slice.

Grill or broil buns to desired doneness.

Spread 1 tbsp. Thousand Island dressing on the bottom half of each bun followed by lettuce, tomato, patty, red onion, and top half of bun.

Makes 4 burgers.

SHEPHERD'S PIE

1 3/4 lbs. lean ground beef
1 large carrot, diced

1 large onion, chopped
salt and pepper to taste
1/2 cup frozen green peas, cooked
1/4 cup frozen corn kernels, cooked
1/3 cup ketchup
1 tsp. sugar
3 large russet potatoes (2 lbs.), peeled and diced
2 tbsp. butter or margarine
2 tbsp. flour
1 cup beef stock
2 tsp. Worcestershire sauce
1 large egg yolk
1/3 cup sour cream
1/3 cup milk
sprinkle paprika
sprinkle dried parsley flakes, optional

In a large frying pan, brown beef over medium-high heat, adding a little olive oil if needed. Add carrot and onion to meat; cook until carrot has softened. Season with salt and pepper. Add cooked peas, corn, ketchup, and sugar and stir to combine.

Bring potatoes to a boil in covered saucepan with salted water. Continue to boil 20 minutes; mash.

Meanwhile, in separate pan, melt butter. Add flour and whisk. Whisk in beef stock and Worcestershire sauce. Pour into meat mixture and combine. Heat on medium-high until thickened. Place in 7" x 11" baking dish.

In large bowl, combine egg yolk, sour cream, and milk. Add to mashed potatoes. Add salt and pepper to taste. Spread over casserole. Sprinkle with paprika.

Heat under broiler (6"–8" from top of oven) to brown, about 5–6 minutes. Keep checking to make sure it's not burning. Sprinkle with parsley if desired.

CRANBERRY POT ROAST

From the story "Lucky's Discovery"

2–2 1/2 lbs. beef round roast, trimmed of fat
2 tsp. cooking oil
1 cup cranberry cocktail
1/2 cup low sodium beef broth
1 tsp. salt
1/2 tsp. dried oregano
1 large onion, chopped
1/4 cup packed brown sugar
1 tsp. salt
3 tbsp. cold water
2 tbsp. cornstarch

Heat oil in a skillet over medium-high heat. Add roast, turning to brown all sides. Remove from heat.

Place meat in roaster and pour juice and broth over top. Add oregano. Sprinkle salt over meat and juice in pan. Roast, covered, at 325° for 1 hour. Stir onions and brown sugar into pan juices. Roast meat, covered, for another 1–1 1/4 hours or until meat and onions are tender. Transfer meat to a serving platter, reserving juices. Cover meat to keep warm.

Strain pan juices, reserving onions. Measure pan juices, adding enough water to measure 2 cups liquid. Pour into saucepan and add the reserved onions. Bring to boiling.

Stir together cold water and cornstarch. Stir into boiling liquid. Cook and stir until thickened and bubbly. Cook and stir 2 minutes more. Serve over meat.

SPAGHETTI AND MEATBALLS

1 large egg
1/4 cup water
1 tsp. salt
1/4 tsp. pepper
1 large onion, finely chopped
1 tsp. garlic powder
1/2 cup bread crumbs
1/2 cup finely grated Parmesan cheese
8 oz. ground pork*
8 oz. ground turkey*
1 tsp. Italian seasoning
1 tbsp. olive oil
28 oz. can crushed tomatoes
3/4 cup water
1 lb. spaghetti

In a large bowl, whisk together egg, 1/4 cup water, salt, and pepper. Stir in half the onion and half the garlic. Add bread crumbs, cheese, meat, and half the Italian seasoning. Mix gently. Form into 16–20 balls.

Heat half the oil in large, non-stick skillet over medium-high heat. Add half the meatballs and brown on all sides, about 4–6 minutes. Transfer to plate with a slotted spoon. Cook remaining meatballs in remaining oil; remove meatballs.

In same skillet, add remaining onion and sauté over medium-low heat until lightly browned and soft, about 5–10 minutes. Add remaining garlic and remaining Italian seasoning and combine. Season with salt and pepper to desired taste. Stir in tomatoes and 3/4 cup water. Return meatballs; cover and simmer until cooked through, about 20 minutes. Remove meatballs.

Cook spaghetti in large pot of boiling water, according to package directions, until al dente. Drain and return to pot. Toss with sauce and then serve meatballs on top, sprinkled with additional Parmesan cheese if desired.

* Note: You can use 1 lb. ground pork or 1 lb. ground turkey instead of a mixture if you prefer. Ground beef can also be substituted.

ITALIAN PASTA BAKE

From the story "Lucky's Discovery"

1 lb. lean ground beef
1 medium onion, chopped
700 ml bottle pasta sauce
1 cup water
1 tsp. sugar
6 lasagna noodles, uncooked (not oven-ready)
1/2 tsp. garlic powder
1/4 tsp. oregano
salt and pepper to taste
2 cups shredded Italiano cheese*
1 cup shredded medium cheddar cheese
2 cups Corn Flakes, crushed to 1 cup crumbs
2 tbsp. butter or margarine, melted

Preheat oven to 375°.

Scramble fry meat with onion and garlic powder over medium-high heat until meat is no longer pink inside; drain and return to skillet. Stir in pasta sauce. Pour water into empty pasta sauce bottle; cover and shake well. Add water, sugar, oregano, salt, and pepper to skillet and combine well. Adding water to sauce helps cook traditional lasagna noodles while baking.
Combine Corn Flake crumbs with melted butter; set aside.

Spray a 7" x 11" baking dish with cooking spray and layer as follows:

1/3 meat sauce
3 uncooked noodles
1/3 meat sauce
cheddar cheese
3 uncooked noodles
remaining meat sauce
Italiano cheese
crumb mixture

Bake, uncovered, 40–45 minutes. Let stand 10 minutes before cutting.

* Another 4-cheese blend can be substituted for Italiano or any white cheese you prefer. A blend containing Parmesan cheese is excellent.

HOLIDAY BISCOTTI

2 cups flour
1 1/2 tsp. baking powder
3/4 cup sugar
1/2 cup unsalted butter, room temperature
1 tsp. grated lemon zest
1/4 tsp. salt
2 large eggs
3/4 cup pistachios, coarsely chopped
2/3 cup dried cranberries
12 oz. good-quality white chocolate, chopped
red and green sugar crystals for garnish

Preheat oven to 350°.

Line a large baking sheet with parchment paper. Whisk the flour and baking powder in a medium bowl to blend. Using an electric mixer, beat the sugar, butter, lemon zest, and salt in a large bowl to blend. Beat in the eggs, one at a time. Add the flour mixture and beat just until blended. Stir in the pistachios and cranberries.

Form the dough into a 13" long x 3" wide log on the prepared baking sheet. Bake until light golden, about 30 minutes. Cool for 30 minutes.

Place the log on a cutting board. Using a sharp serrated knife, cut the log on a diagonal into 1/2 to 3/4 inch thick slices. Arrange the biscotti, cut side down, on the baking sheet. Bake until they are pale golden, about 13 minutes. Transfer the biscotti to a rack and cool completely.

Melt chocolate in a bowl over simmering water or in microwave, making sure not to overcook. Dip one end of the biscotti into the melted chocolate up about halfway. Gently shake off the excess chocolate. Place the biscotti on the baking sheet for the chocolate to set. Sprinkle with the sugar crystals. Refrigerate until the chocolate is firm, about 35 minutes.

The biscotti can be made ahead. Store them in an airtight container up to 4 days or wrap them in foil and freeze in resealable plastic bags up to 3 weeks.

BLUEBERRY CAKE AND RUM SAUCE

Cake:

1/2 cup butter or hard margarine
1 cup sugar
1 egg
2 cups flour
3 tsp. baking powder
1/2 tsp salt
3/4 cup milk
1 tsp. vanilla
1 1/4 cups blueberries, dusted with flour

Preheat oven to 350°.

Cream butter and sugar with electric mixer. Add egg and vanilla and beat well.

Combine flour, baking powder, and salt. Beat into butter mixture alternately with milk, until creamed. Gently stir in berries (dusting them first with flour prevents them from sinking to the bottom).

Pour into a greased 8" square baking dish. Bake 35–40 minutes, until toothpick inserted in centre comes out clean. Cool.

Rum Sauce:

2 cups water
1/3 cup butter or hard margarine
1/2 cup brown sugar
2 tsp. vanilla
1 tsp. rum flavouring
pinch salt
1/2 cup water
2 rounded tbsp. cornstarch

Combine first 6 ingredients in small saucepan and bring to a boil. Stir together second amount of water and cornstarch. Add to sauce until desired thickness is reached. Serve hot over blueberry cake.

CHOCOLATE ERUPTIONS

2 tsp. butter or hard margarine
cocoa powder
2/3 cup butter or hard margarine
5 - 1 oz. squares semi-sweet baking chocolate, chopped
2 tsp. vanilla
2 large eggs and 2 yolks
1 1/2 cups icing sugar
1/2 cup flour
6 scoops vanilla ice cream

Preheat oven to 450°.

Grease bottoms and sides of six 6 oz. ramekins with first amount of butter. Dust each dish with about 1/2 tsp. or so of cocoa powder to completely cover bottoms and sides. Discard excess powder.

In small, heavy saucepan, heat second amount of butter, chocolate, and vanilla on very low heat, stirring often, until chocolate has almost melted. Do not overheat. Remove from heat and stir until smooth. Cool slightly.

In medium bowl, beat eggs and egg yolks for about 2 minutes, until frothy. On low speed, beat in icing sugar, then chocolate mixture, and flour. Beat until thick and frothy. Divide batter among ramekins and place on baking sheet.

Bake 12 minutes, until edges are set, but middle is still wobbly. Let stand 5 minutes. Cut around edges with a knife to loosen cakes. Cover each dish with a small plate and invert. Serve immediately or keep cakes warm in ramekins for 15–20 minutes before removing.

Serve each cake with a scoop of softened ice cream. For garnish, a dusting of icing sugar may be added to cake and a dusting of cocoa powder to ice cream.

An eruption of gooey chocolate will burst forth when cut into.

PISTACHIO DESSERT

1 cup flour
1/2 cup butter or margarine
1/2 cup finely chopped pecans
8 oz. cream cheese, softened

1 cup icing sugar
1 pkg. instant pistachio pudding mix
1 3/4 cups milk
1 cup whipping cream
3 tbsp. sliced almonds

Preheat oven to 350°.

Mix flour and butter together until crumbly. Stir in pecans and press into an ungreased 9" x 13" baking pan. Bake 15 minutes. Cool.

Beat cream cheese and sugar together until well combined. Spread over cooled shortbread crust.

Beat pudding mix with milk and pour over cream cheese layer. Chill until firm.

Whip cream until stiff. Spread over pudding layer and sprinkle with almonds. Keep chilled.

ICE CREAM BROWNIE DESSERT

1 pkg. Supreme Chocolate Chunk Brownie Mix
water, vegetable oil, and egg called for on brownie package
1 cup Skor toffee bits
6 cups vanilla ice cream, softened
1/2 cup soft whipped chocolate frosting

Preheat oven to 350°.

Prepare brownies according to package directions. Spread in a 9" x 13" pan, greased on bottom only. Bake 22–25 minutes. Do not over-bake. Cool completely.

Stir toffee bits into ice cream. Spoon over cooled brownie base, smoothing top.

In small saucepan over low heat, melt frosting. Stir well. Drizzle over ice cream. Freeze 2 hours or until firm. Thaw 10 minutes before cutting into bars.

PEPPERMINT CHEESECAKE

1 cup chocolate wafer crumbs
3 tbsp. butter or hard margarine, melted
1 envelope unflavoured gelatin
1/4 cup cold water
2 - 8 oz. pkgs. cream cheese, softened
1/2 cup sugar
1/2 cup 2% evaporated milk
1/4 cup crushed candy canes
1 cup whipping cream, whipped
3 oz. milk chocolate candy bar, chopped
additional grated chocolate for garnish if desired
additional crushed candy canes for garnish if desired

Preheat oven to 350°.

Combine crumbs and butter and press into the bottom of a 9" springform pan. Bake 10 minutes. Cool.

Soften gelatin in water and stir over low heat until dissolved.

Beat cream cheese with sugar on medium speed of electric mixer until blended well. Gradually beat in gelatin, milk, and crushed candy canes. Place in freezer 10 minutes to thicken, but not to completely set. Fold in whipped cream and chopped chocolate bar. Garnish with grated chocolate and additional crushed candy canes if desired. Chill to set.

CHOCOLATE COOKIE CHEESECAKE

From the story "A Paramedic's Nightmare"
3 - 8 oz. pkgs cream cheese
3/4 cup sugar
3 eggs
1 tsp. vanilla
1 cup sour cream
2 tsp. flour
15 Oreo cookies, broken*

Crust:

1 3/4 cups Oreo crumbs
3 tbsp. melted butter or margarine
1/8 cup sugar

Combine Oreo crumbs, melted butter, and 1/8 cup sugar. Press into bottom and 1/4 way up sides of a lightly greased 8" or 9" springform pan. Refrigerate.

In bowl, beat cream cheese. Beat in 3/4 cup sugar until fluffy. Beat in eggs, one at a time, beating well after each addition; beat in vanilla, sour cream and flour.

Pour 1/3 cream cheese mixture over prepared crust. Sprinkle with half the broken cookies. Repeat once. Top with remaining batter, smoothing top.

Bake in 325° oven for 1 hour or until edge is set, but centre still jiggles slightly. Turn oven off. Let cool in oven 1 hour. Let cool completely on rack. Cover and refrigerate overnight or up to three days.

* Instead of breaking up regular Oreo cookies, whole Mini Oreos can be substituted. Additional whipped topping and mini Oreo cookies make a great garnish for the top.

EGGNOG

12 eggs, separated
1 cup sugar
1 quart milk
1 cup whipping cream
1 cup brandy or spiced rum

Beat egg yolks slightly. Add sugar, a little at a time, and continue beating until smooth. Pour in milk and brandy. Stir until well mixed.

Beat egg whites until soft peaks form. In separate bowl, beat whipping cream until firm. Fold whites and whipping cream into yolk mixture. Add a few ice cubes to keep chilled. Sprinkle with nutmeg.

PINK FRUIT PUNCH

4 cups pineapple juice
4 cups cranberry cocktail
2 tbsp. lemon juice
9 cups ginger ale
2 1/2 cups vodka
2 cups gin

Combine first 3 ingredients in punch bowl and chill if not serving right away. Just before serving, add ginger ale, vodka, and gin. Garnish with lemon and lime slices. Add ice cubes or an ice ring to keep chilled.

PINEAPPLE-ORANGE PUNCH

8 cups orange juice
4 cups unsweetened pineapple juice
2 tbsp. lemon juice
4 cups lemon-lime soft drink
4 cups vodka

Combine first 3 ingredients in large punch bowl and chill until ready to serve. Just before serving, add soft drink and vodka. Garnish with orange and lime slices and cherries if desired. Add ice cubes or ice ring to keep it chilled.

BRUNCH CUPS

From the story "Snowbound"

3 cups cooked rice

1/2 cup shredded Cheddar cheese

4 oz. diced green chilies

2 oz. diced pimientos, drained

1/3 cup skim milk

2 eggs, beaten

1/4 tsp. ground cumin

1/2 tsp. salt

1/4 tsp. pepper

1/2 cup shredded cheddar cheese

Preheat oven to 400°.

In a large bowl, combine first 9 ingredients. Divide mixture among 12 muffin cups that have been sprayed with cooking spray. Sprinkle with remaining cheese.

Bake 15 minutes. Makes 12.

SALT-FREE SPICE

5 tsp. onion powder

2 tsp. garlic powder

2 1/2 tsp. paprika

2 1/2 tsp. dry mustard

1/2 tsp. dried thyme

1/2 tsp. white pepper

1/2 tsp. celery seed

Combine all ingredients well. Store in a spice bottle or covered jar. Makes about 1/3 cup.

About the Authors

Lisa Ivany lives in Gander and works full-time as a psychiatric secretary and part-time as an orthopaedic executive assistant at the James Paton Memorial Hospital. When not working or writing, she loves to cook, walk, read, and cross-stitch. She welcomes feedback on her writing and invites readers to email her at livany@nf.sympatico.ca.

Robert Hunt lives in St. John's and is employed at the St. John's International Airport. His pleasures in life include his first love, writing, reading, sports, and jogging. Like his co-author, he also enjoys hearing from readers and can be contacted at bobhunt99@yahoo.ca.